# *LOVE'S GENTLE SEASON*

LAURA PARRISH

*AVALON BOOKS*
THOMAS BOUREGY AND COMPANY, INC.
401 LAFAYETTE STREET
NEW YORK, NEW YORK 10003

© Copyright 1989 by Laura Parrish
Library of Congress Catalog Card Number: 89-60807
ISBN 0-8034-8757-6
All rights reserved.
All the characters in this book are fictitious,
and any resemblance to actual persons,
living or dead, is purely coincidental.

PRINTED IN THE UNITED STATES OF AMERICA
BY HADDON CRAFTSMEN, SCRANTON, PENNSYLVANIA

To my husband, Lewis, with love

## Chapter One

"I'm sorry you and Dad don't approve of my plan, Mother. But I'm still going to do it." Jamie Richards's voice was firm and sure, but her hand tightened on the telephone receiver until the knuckles showed starkly white against her tan.

She listened for a few moments longer, then said good-bye and replaced the phone on its stand. Her hazel eyes stormy, she sat for a while, drumming her fingers on the desktop.

A few minutes ago, she'd been happy and excited, eager to tell her parents about the wonderful chance her grandmother had offered her. She should have known what their reaction would be.

She sighed and tucked a lock of her sun-streaked light brown hair behind her ear. They hadn't been able to understand what made her tick since she was twelve years old and had become horse crazy. They'd finally given in and bought her a gelding, and she'd spent every spare moment from then on at the stables where Dusty was boarded, grooming him, feeding him, learning to ride.

As young as she'd been, she'd known what she wanted to do with her life, but she hadn't dared to tell her family. Beatrice and Philip Richards were very successful corporate attorneys in Atlanta. Her sister, Linda, ten years older, was already a junior partner in the firm. Jamie knew they expected her to carry on the family tradition and become a lawyer too.

So Jamie had dutifully made good grades all through high school and three years of college, grateful she could live at home and still continue her daily visits to the stables. But after her junior year in college, she knew she couldn't go on with it—not to please her parents, not for anything. College itself was interesting enough, since Jamie was very bright, but she couldn't face the life for which it was preparing her.

How had she ever thought she could stand being stuck practicing law in a stuffy office? The whole concept was totally foreign to her. She just couldn't do it.

She finished her junior year, then dropped her bombshell on her unsuspecting parents and stood firm under their barrage of arguments. She hated to disappoint them, but it was her life, after all. She had to do with it what would make her happy, and what she was suited for.

Ted Davis, the boy she'd met that year, fallen in love with, and become engaged to, was equally horrified. Ted was a premed student, programmed for success. He refused to go along with her decision. If she was going to do this crazy thing, their engagement was over, he told her, obviously expecting her to capitulate at his ultimatum.

Instead, Jamie had given him his ring back with a heavy heart. She'd been so sure Ted would understand, since she'd talked so often to him about her dreams. But he just hadn't taken her seriously, she saw now.

That summer she had found a job on a horse farm, to learn the business from the ground up. She had moved from her parents' beautiful house in suburban Atlanta to central Florida, taking Dusty with her. She'd scrimped and saved, and now, three years later, her grandmother's wonderful offer had come. Elinor Scott wanted to retire from farming, but she also wanted to keep living in the place that had been her home since her marriage.

She'd offered to sell Jamie her hundred-acre farm in the West Florida Panhandle, giving her a long-term mortgage if Jamie would let her continue to live there, terms that Jamie had been delighted to accept. At last her dreams were coming true. If only her family could share them with her.

Jamie sighed again, then firmly pushed her chair back and stood, her face brightening. She wouldn't let their disapproval spoil her happiness. And now she had to get busy and pack.

Excitement tingled through Jamie's veins as she drove her pickup truck west on I-10, pulling the horse trailer with Dusty inside. The passing scenery was gradually changing from semitropical central Florida's tall palms to western Florida's pines, scrub oaks, and palmettos.

She'd always loved her grandparents' farm, tucked away in its secluded spot. Now the area was building up, and the farm wasn't so secluded anymore. In fact, except for her grandmother's land and the acreage bordering it, most of the other farmland had been sold to developers and was already dotted with houses. She frowned as she thought about the one remaining farm next to Elinor Scott's.

The farmer who'd owned it during Jamie's growing-up years had sold it to a younger man—Matt Douglas. Ever since Mr. Douglas had bought his land, he'd been trying to buy her grandmother's farm, to extend his holdings. Elinor hadn't promised him anything, but maybe her grandmother had encouraged him a little, Jamie worried, before she knew Jamie would be thrilled to accept her generous offer.

Jamie wondered if Matt Douglas would be a problem in her renovation of the farm. She hoped any resentment he felt over not being able to buy the farm wouldn't extend to her. It would be much nicer to have friendly neighbors.

Her anticipation grew as she got closer, and by the time she turned off the interstate onto the county road, she could hardly wait to get there. Her own land and her own horse stables! Her own dream come true at last!

Elinor Scott was sitting on the wide front veranda in a rocking chair with her dog, Prince, beside her when Jamie pulled up in the drive. Prince lifted his head when he heard the truck, then got to his feet. As she saw the delighted smile on her grandmother's face, Jamie gave her an answering smile. Trailed by the dog, the older woman rose and walked toward the truck.

As Jamie got out and closed the truck door behind her, the summer heat and humidity hit her. But it wasn't as bad as in central Florida, she thought. Here there was nearly always a breeze off the nearby bay. "Oh, Gram! It's great to be here." She gave her grandmother an exuberant hug, which was vigorously returned. Elinor Scott may have wanted to retire, but she was still strong and active.

"It's so good to have you here, honey."

"Hi, Prince old boy." Jamie patted the dog's head. A twinge of sadness hit her as she saw his almost-white muzzle. He whined, lifting his front paw, as he'd been doing since he was a puppy. Jamie laughed and took his paw.

"Did Phil and Bea raise much of a ruckus when you told them?" Elinor pushed back a strand of her graying hair, and smiled fondly at her granddaughter.

Jamie made a face. "Did they ever! Especially Mother. You'd think I'd told her I planned to start a career of bank robbing!"

Elinor grinned. "Bet they're blaming me for selling to you too, aren't they?"

Jamie returned her grin, but her happiness dimmed for a minute. "Sort of, I guess. They think we're both crazy."

Elinor's smile turned rueful. "I guess they have as hard a time understanding us as I always did trying to figure out Bea. She was so different from John and me. Bea always wanted to get out of the country and into a city."

"I must be a throwback to you and

Grandpa." Jamie walked to the back of the horse trailer. "Dusty is as glad to be here as I am. I'd better take him out to the fields."

Elinor looked through the slats at the buckskin gelding. "He must be pretty old by now, isn't he, Jamie? You've had him a long time."

"Since I was twelve." Jamie smiled fondly. "But he was only four when I got him, so he's just sixteen now. He'll make a good horse for trail rides and lessons."

"Yes, that will save you some money. You can put him in the small field behind the barn. That fence is in good shape. Can't say the same for all of them, though."

In a few minutes, Jamie had unloaded Dusty in the field, and he was contentedly grazing. Her grandparents had made an automatic waterer for their horses out of an old discarded bathtub, as was common practice. But, unused for years, it no longer worked, she discovered. She was confident she could fix it tomorrow, but in the meantime she had to bring a small metal tub out from the barn and fill it with water.

She walked around, looking at the different kinds of wild grasses. All of them here were safe for Dusty, but she'd have to check the other fields before she turned him into them. She'd also have to do some fence repairing, but this field would be big enough for one horse, as long as they had enough rain.

Her grandmother was waiting at the yard fence for her. Jamie linked her arm in the older woman's as they walked toward the white-painted house. "Do you have any iced tea? I'm parched."

Elinor squeezed her granddaughter's arm. "I just made a fresh pitcher and baked some brownies. Come on, we'll have a snack."

As she followed her grandmother to the front door, Jamie looked with new eyes at the old place, now that it was going to be hers. Yes, she hadn't made a bad move, in spite of what her parents thought. It would do just fine.

The house needed only minor repairs. Her grandparents had been careful about upkeep. It was just in the last five years, since Grandpa John had died, that it had started looking a little shabby.

She couldn't see the big barn from here, but she knew it inside out. It, too, was a little run down, but she could do most of the repairs herself, she thought, with the help of a local handyman. The biggest job would be putting up new fences and fixing the existing ones.

Inside the wide front hall it was much cooler, even without air-conditioning. Her parents and sister wouldn't visit in the summer because of what they termed her grandmother's stubbornness about installing central air-conditioning. "Can't stand to be shut up in the house all summer!" she'd heard her grandmother protest, and Jamie really couldn't blame her.

All the rooms had lazily rotating ceiling fans, which kept the air circulating. The house's thick walls also helped. And there were window air conditioners in the bedrooms upstairs for the sultry nights.

Taking a delighted breath, Jamie followed her grandmother to the big, old-fashioned kitchen. Jamie loved this room, and wouldn't do a thing to change it. A round oak table dominated the square room, and Elinor's maple rocker still stood in front of the side window.

Elinor took the pitcher of tea from the refrigerator and filled a plate with brownies from a cookie jar by the stove. Jamie washed her hands at the sink, then got two of the amber-colored glasses from the cabinet shelf where they'd stood ever since she could remember.

Soon Jamie and Elinor were both sitting at the table, their glasses of tea in front of them, the brownies in the middle of the table. "I can't believe you're here to stay, Jamie, instead of just to visit." Elinor beamed at her granddaughter.

Jamie smiled back widely. "Neither can I. Oh, Gram, it's so wonderful to be here! I can hardly wait to get started!"

Elinor laughed. "I know just how you feel. I was that way when your grandpa and I moved here. Every day was a new adventure. We can look around the place this evening, and you can see what you need to buy for repairs and such." She paused, and her face became serious. "Are you sure you want to tackle this, honey?" She looked searchingly at Jamie.

Jamie nodded vigorously. "I've never been so sure of anything in my life. I've been working toward my own place for years, Gram. But I didn't dream I'd get this one. I thought you'd never want to sell it."

"I didn't, but I can't keep it up anymore. Sometimes I think I've taken advantage of you. Not too many buyers would let the previous owner stay on." Elinor smiled, but her snapping dark eyes were still serious.

Jamie's full lips firmed, and her dark-lashed hazel eyes looked straight at her grandmother. "I wouldn't have it any other way," she said. Then her mouth softened and curved into a smile. "Besides, I've never learned to cook, and you're the best cook I know."

Elinor's face relaxed as her smile broadened. "Oh, so you have an ulterior motive, do you?"

"Oh." This put a new light on the matter, and Jamie felt relieved. Her grandmother had said Matt Douglas was young—but, then, to Elinor anyone under fifty was young. If he'd already managed to be that successful, he must be middle-aged, anyway.

## Love's Gentle Season

Jamie nodded again. "You bet! You'll have to give me cooking lessons, but it might take a long time for me to learn, what with all the outside work I have to do."

"I don't think that will be too big a problem." The older woman lifted her glass of tea, and pushed the plate of brownies toward Jamie. "Here, help yourself. You look as if you need a little fattening up."

Jamie groaned as she took two of the delectably rich treats. "It won't take long if you keep on baking these. There's one thing I wanted to find out, Gram. Since he wanted to buy the place, is this Matt Douglas going to be hard for me to get along with?"

Elinor looked surprised, as if she'd never considered this problem. "Why, I don't think so, Jamie. Matt's a really reasonable man. He didn't seem to have any hard feelings about it when I told him. After all, he could understand that I'd sell to my granddaughter before anyone else."

But for some reason, Jamie still felt a little uneasy. "Still, it must have been a real disappointment, since there isn't much land left around here besides yours that he could buy."

"Matt's already got a big ranch near Ocala. I think he just wants to live here part of the time, and raise a few horses as a sideline."

## Chapter Two

*A* trickle of perspiration slid under Jamie's sweatband into her eyes, and she narrowly missed hitting her thumb with the hammer clenched in her right hand. Her left held a large nail against the board with which she was patching a stall. "Oh, blast!" she muttered, swiping at her face.

Why had she ever thought the Panhandle wasn't as hot and humid as central Florida? If it got much hotter, she was going to have a heatstroke. Her grandmother had offered to help, but it was just too hot to allow her. And Jamie wanted to save her limited funds for hired help until she started work on the fences.

The board had slipped out of position. Jamie bit her lower lip as she painstakingly moved it upward again. "What I need are two more hands," she muttered to herself.

"I have a couple I can lend you." The deep male voice came out of nowhere, and then a shadow momentarily blocked out the light as a large tanned hand grasped the sliding board and held it firmly in place.

Jamie whirled, so startled she almost dropped the hammer. She drew in her breath sharply, and her eyes widened as she took in the man smiling easily at her. No wonder he'd blocked the light. He must be well over six feet tall, long legged and lean in jeans, his shoulders stretching the blue T-shirt he wore. His hair, under the Western-style straw hat, was black, his eyes a deep blue, with crinkly laugh lines at the corners.

Jamie realized her mouth was hanging open. Embarrassed, she closed it firmly, and managed a small smile of her own. He must be an acquaintance of her grandmother's, or Prince would never have let him get this far. "That's a dangerous thing to say. I may keep you here all day."

The man shrugged his wide shoulders, his smile lingering. "That's all right. I'm not too busy today. Would you like me to do the hammering, and you the holding?"

Jamie didn't hesitate long. If one of her grandmother's friends had stopped by and seemed willing—almost eager—to help, she wouldn't turn him down. She extended the hammer, her smile widening. "That's the best offer I've had all day."

His hand brushed hers as he took the hammer, and Jamie was startled at the tingle that went up her spine at the brief contact. She'd been too busy the last three years to do much dating, and Ted's defection had left her feeling disillusioned and a little wary of men.

While Jamie held the board, the man nailed it in place with strong, accurate hammer strokes. Jamie handed him another board to place below it, and he started again.

"I just stopped by to welcome you, and Elly told me you were out working," he said. "I'm Matt Douglas, your neighbor."

Matt Douglas! Jamie's hand slipped, and she almost lost her grip on the board. All her ideas about him did an abrupt about-face. This extremely attractive man couldn't be over thirty.

She took a deep breath and got a grip on herself. "I'm Jamie Richards, as I guess you know." Her voice sounded a little stiff, she noticed. She cleared her throat and tried again. "I'm glad to meet you, but I didn't expect neighborliness to go this far."

"Oh, we all help each other around here. You never know when you're going to need help yourself." Matt's deep voice, with its hint of a drawl, sounded unperturbed. He drove the last nail into the second board, and she handed him the third one, which would complete the repairs on this stall.

Soon they were finished, and Matt stood back to look at the stall. "Not too bad a job," he said. "This old barn was made of good solid stuff. It's worth fixing up."

"Yes, that's what I thought too." Jamie felt pleased at his approval, as if her own judgment had been validated, then was annoyed at herself. It was bad enough that she constantly had to prove herself to her parents. She didn't have to with this man, no matter how nice and attractive he was. He was only her neighbor, after all.

Just as her grandmother had said, he didn't seem upset with her for buying the property he'd wanted. Or he kept his feelings well hidden. But his handsome face was open and candid. He didn't seem the type for harboring secrets.

"Lunch is ready—and you need to get in out of this heat for a while." Elinor stood in the barn doorway. "Matt, you come on in too. I've got sandwiches and salad—plenty for us all."

"You talked me into it, Elly—especially if you've got some iced tea." Matt gave the older woman a warm smile.

"I always keep a pitcher in the fridge—you know that." Elinor grinned back at him.

*Love's Gentle Season* 17

In a few minutes, they were all seated around the oak table, frosty glasses of tea and bowls of crisp salad in front of them. Chicken sandwiches filled a plate in the middle of the table. Matt seemed perfectly at home. He and Elinor were good friends, Jamie could see. He'd obviously been kind to her grandmother, and he'd helped her finish a hard job. She should be glad of that.

She was, Jamie assured herself. She had absolutely no reason to regard him with suspicion, and she wouldn't. He had nothing to gain by being nice. He was just doing it because he wanted to.

"So you're going to settle down in the Panhandle." Matt turned to Jamie with a smile.

Jamie forced herself to relax and smile back. "I stayed with Gram on school vacations quite a lot. I've always loved this area. It has a feeling of being really far out in the country, and yet we're only a few miles from the bay."

Matt nodded as he forked up another bite of salad. "Yes, that's what I like about it too. If I could find some more land, I'd expand my horse-breeding operations here."

Jamie gave him a sharp glance as she lifted her glass of tea. Was he hinting that she'd spoiled his chances to acquire the land here?

He gave her a slow smile that did funny

things to her pulse rate. "I've got my eye on a nice plot a little farther west. If I don't get it"—he shrugged—"then I'll just use this as my retreat."

"Do you breed horses here?" His last statement had made Jamie relax a little.

Matt nodded. "In a small way. I've got a champion quarter-horse stud, and I'd like to see what he can do."

Jamie's eyes began to shine. Any kind of horse talk excited her. "That's my dream too, eventually. Of course, first I have to get my stables off the ground."

"Are you going to run boarding stables?" Matt's blue eyes lingered on her animated face.

Jamie nodded happily. "Yes, and give riding lessons. I've got enough money to buy another gelding for that and a mare to start my own stock."

"I've got a nice little mare you might be interested in. A chestnut quarter horse. She comes with a bonus—she's in foal."

"From your stud?" Jamie asked, her eyes shining with interest.

"Yes, and she's a beauty," Elinor put in, passing around the salad bowl. "You do mean Misty, don't you, Matt?"

"Yes. She's had two other foals—both with good lines."

"I didn't know you planned to sell her," Elinor commented.

Matt shrugged. "Her last foal was out of Smoke—I know what she can do, combined with him. I've got my eye on another mare over at Hartsell's."

Jamie's eager excitement faded as she gave Matt another sharp glance. Had he made this offer out of charity? Because he knew she was operating on a shoestring? If so, she wanted nothing to do with it! She was going to stand on her own two feet, sink or swim.

"She won't come cheap." Matt seemed to be reading her mind. "But she doesn't have to be paid for all at once. In any case, you haven't even looked at her. You might not like her at all."

Jamie swallowed as she returned his even glance. "I'd like to take a look at her."

"Fine. Do you want to come on back with me now? It's too hot to do any more carpentry work until evening."

"Yes, why don't you do that, honey?" Elinor urged. "I know you'll fall in love with Misty. She's gentle, but spirited too. And a little beauty."

Her grandparents had raised horses years ago, and Jamie knew her grandmother was a good judge of horseflesh. The older woman's urging decided her. She pushed back her chair, just as Matt did. She gave him a warm smile. "All right, that sounds like a good idea."

As she walked to the door, Matt close behind her, she felt the magnetic pull of his masculinity. Her excitement rose again, singing in her veins. The long summer stretched before her, to be filled with work so satisfying it would be pure pleasure. A summer full of magic.

"You may as well go with me—no use taking two vehicles." Matt fell in beside Jamie. His mud-spattered Jeep was parked in the driveway beside the house.

"Then you'd have to bring me back. I wouldn't want to inconvenience you," Jamie said quickly, realizing she felt a little nervous about being alone with him in the small confines of the Jeep.

He gave her his slow smile again. "It's no trouble. I don't live that far away."

Jamie decided she was being ridiculous. She shrugged. "All right." She followed him to the Jeep, and slid inside after Matt opened the passenger door. The small courtesy made her feel absurdly feminine. She wasn't used to such things. On the horse farm, she'd been treated just like the boys and men who worked there, given no special treatment because she was a female. She'd wanted it that way of course—but, still, this was nice.

Matt backed the Jeep onto the gravel road in front of the house and turned right. "Your grandmother is really something. She's like a woman half her age." He broke the small silence that had fallen between them, his voice easy and casual. He certainly didn't seem to feel any constraint.

And neither did she, Jamie told herself firmly. "Yes, she is. I always wished I could have lived with her all the time when I was growing up, instead of just a few weeks during summer vacation. She always let me be as much of a tomboy as I wanted to be."

Matt chuckled. "I take it your parents didn't approve of that?"

Evidently her grandmother hadn't told Matt about her family's disapproval of her plans for the stables. Jamie shook her head. "That's the understatement of the century. They think I've lost my mind by buying this place." She'd planned to keep her voice light and careless, but she heard the edge in her words that she couldn't stop.

Matt must have heard it too. He gave her a quick glance, then turned back to his driving. "They don't like country life, then?"

Jamie made a wry face. "Nope. My father

was born and raised in Atlanta, and my mother headed there as soon as she finished high school. They're city people through and through. Of course, there wouldn't be all that much law business out here, I'll have to admit."

"Elinor told me your parents and sister are partners in a law firm." Matt's voice was carefully neutral as he turned left again, onto a lane that wound away between live oaks and magnolias.

Jamie nodded, feeling tension rising in her at the way the conversation was going. "Yes," she said, trying to keep her feelings from showing. "I was supposed to finish up the pattern. I don't think they'll ever forgive me for choosing another life-style."

Matt turned one final bend in the lane, then pulled up before a magnificent house, all stone and cedar and huge glass windows. "Here we are," he announced.

Jamie breathed a sigh of relief that he'd dropped the talk about her family. She stared in fascination at the house. She hadn't expected anything like this. "What a wonderful house!"

Matt gazed at it for a minute before opening his door. "It's what I've always wanted—my dream house, I guess you could say. I never had time to build one in the Ocala area, where

*Love's Gentle Season* 23

the ranch is. I was too busy building up the business. When I bought this place, I decided the time was finally right."

He talked as if he'd done the actual construction, Jamie thought. Well, he knew how to use a hammer, she had to admit. He'd proved that today. "Did you help build it?" she asked.

He shrugged. "A good bit. That was another thing I'd always wanted to do." He opened his door and got out.

Jamie quickly opened her door, and slid out too. She glimpsed a big barn across an open field behind the house. "I'd like to do that too."

Matt stepped up beside her, smiling. "You're pretty handy with a hammer," he said, echoing her own thoughts of a moment ago. "No reason why you couldn't."

Jamie felt an unexpected surge of elation. Except for her grandmother, no one had ever talked to her like this before—as if she could do anything she wanted to. She gave Matt a wide smile. "Maybe I'll do that—when my stables become a big success," she finished half mockingly.

Matt's look turned serious. "I think that will happen too, Jamie," he said quietly. "You're smart and capable, and know the horse business, Elinor tells me."

Jamie's elation changed into that warm, tingly feeling she'd experienced earlier when she first met Matt. She felt her wariness return. She wasn't quite ready to trust any man yet. "Well, thanks for the vote of confidence," she said lightly. "Now, where's that mare?"

"Right this way." Matt's tone, too, had returned to casualness as he led the way to a metal farm gate and opened it. "I don't see her out here, so she's probably in the barn."

Jamie followed him across a field, admiring the lush grass. Matt evidently knew how to take care of pastureland. The barn was new too, she saw, as they approached it, new and well built. As with the house, there had been no stinting on expenses. She felt a small pang of envy. It must be nice to be able to build just what you wanted, with no worry about how much it cost.

The barn was shadowed and cooler than the outside. Matt walked down the center aisle to a stall near the end. Most of the stalls were empty, Jamie saw. She stopped beside him, her eyes going to the mare standing by her feed box. "Oh, she's a beauty!"

Matt laughed. "You sound surprised. Did you think I was fixin' to sell you a mule?"

Jamie laughed, too, at his sudden lapse into colloquialism. "No, of course not. But she's a

## Love's Gentle Season

dandy! Look at that head! Does she have some Arab blood?"

"Misty's a registered quarter horse, but maybe there's some Arabian back there somewhere."

"Is she skittish?" Jamie moved slowly up behind Matt, so as not to startle the mare.

"Nope, gentle as a lamb. That's one reason I wanted to breed her to Smoke, my stud, again. He's very gentle too. They should produce a good foal, like the last one."

Reassured, Jamie walked up to the mare, and gently rubbed the velvety nose. The mare nuzzled into Jamie's palm. Jamie laughed. "I believe she's looking for a treat."

Matt laughed too. "You're right. I usually bring along a carrot or an apple."

"Oh, you little beauty," Jamie crooned, continuing to caress the mare's shining, dark brown coat. "I think we'll get along just fine."

"I think so too." Matt was close behind her. She could feel his warm breath on her neck. "She likes you. She's friendly with everyone, but she can tell you know horses." His voice sounded admiring and approving.

Jamie felt a warm glow go through her again. Her employers and fellow workers on the horse farm had considered her a good worker, but that somehow wasn't the same as having Matt's approval. *What is the matter with you, Jamie Richards?* she asked herself, dropping her hand, and stepping back. *You've just met this man today. You don't even know him.*

"Well, I'm sold on her. I'm ready to talk business," she said briskly.

After a moment's silence, Matt said, "Good. I know you'll like each other." His own voice had changed back into a more casual tone, the warmth and intimacy of a moment ago gone, as if he sensed Jamie's withdrawal.

Jamie felt a moment of loss, as if she'd stamped on a small, delicate budding thing. *Don't be ridiculous,* she scolded herself. *If there's one thing you don't want to do, it's rush into any kind of a relationship. You did that with Ted, and look what happened. You didn't even know him, and you thought you were madly in love with him!*

And it was the height of conceit for her to imagine that Matt was interested in her as anything more than a friendly neighbor. With one last look at the mare, she followed him out of the barn.

## Chapter Three

"A letter from your mother." Elinor opened the kitchen screen and came inside, waving an envelope. "She always calls, never writes. Wonder what's on her mind."

Jamie, putting away the last of the lunch dishes, watched as her grandmother tore open the envelope, a sinking feeling in her stomach. She could guess why her mother had written. No doubt she was trying to feel her grandmother out about the success or failure of Jamie's business. Or, as Bea Richards always put it, "Jamie's little project."

Jamie clenched her teeth, thinking about that telephone call the day she'd come here, two weeks ago. Her mother hadn't called or written her since, and Jamie knew how upset she'd left her. Was this an olive branch extended—to her grandmother first?

Elinor, reading the letter, snorted. "Ha, Bea hasn't changed a bit. Listen to this: 'Mother dear, Philip, Linda, and I are planning to visit you as soon as the weather cools down. You

27

know we can't stand it out there when it's so hot. Now, if you'd just be reasonable, and let us put in central air-conditioning for you.'"

Jamie, listening, was stung to the quick. Her mother made no reference to Jamie's presence, no acknowledgment that the farm now belonged to her. She turned sharply away, tears stinging her eyelids until she could hardly see the silverware she was putting away.

She felt her grandmother's hand on her shoulder. "Honey, don't let them get you down. You know how they are. All of us have got a streak of stubbornness a mile wide. You do too, you know; you just show it differently."

Jamie blinked and swiped at her face, then turned to give her grandmother a wavery smile. "You're right, Gram. I shouldn't expect anything else. They still think I'm going to come to my senses and finish college and go to law school."

Elinor grinned at her granddaughter. "And are you?" she challenged.

"No!" Jamie tilted her chin in the air. "I'm going to prove to them that I can make a go of this place!"

"Atta girl," her grandmother said approvingly. "How many stalls do you have repaired now?"

"Six," Jamie answered. "Besides Misty's

*Love's Gentle Season* 29

and Dusty's, I mean. I'm about ready to start advertising for boarders and lessons. I should try to find another gelding too."

The older woman nodded. "What about the fences? Is Matt going to help you with them?"

Jamie bit her lip. "I don't think so, Gram. I can't keep on letting him help me so much. He must have work of his own he needs to do. I don't want anybody feeling sorry for me."

Elinor shook her head. "Still got that chip on your shoulder, don't you, girl? Matt doesn't feel the least bit sorry for you—you ought to know that. Where are your eyes?"

Jamie felt her face reddening. "Gram, don't start any matchmaking," she warned. "Matt's not interested in being anything but a friend. And neither am I," she ended firmly.

"Uh-huh, I hear you." Her grandmother gave her a sideways smile, and turned away. "Come on, let's go out to the barn. I haven't seen the horses for a while. How's Misty doing?"

Jamie hung up the dish towel and followed Elinor out the door. "Fine. She's settled down as though she's been here all her life."

"There's good blood in that mare," Elinor said, as they walked along side by side. "Her last foal was a beauty. She should throw another good one."

* * *

"Hi, Steve. How are things going?" Jamie walked into the feed store and smiled at the teenager behind the counter.

"Okay, Jamie." He gave her a wide smile. "Need some more sweet feed already?"

Jamie shook her head. "No, I'm not after feed today. I just wondered if I could leave these here, and maybe you could give them to the customers." She set a stack of fliers down on the battered wooden countertop.

Steve picked up one and read it. "Hey, how about that! You're ready to take boarders and give riding lessons, huh?"

Jamie nodded. "At long last. I still don't have all the fences up, but I can start with one or two boarders, anyway. And I bought another gelding for giving lessons last week. Maybe I can make a little money while I keep fixing up. Do you think your dad would mind if I left the fliers here?"

Steve evened the stack, giving her another eager smile. "Nah. Dad won't care. Somebody's always leaving something like this. Want me to put a couple in the front windows too?"

"Oh, that would be great, Steve." Jamie gave him a warm smile, and saw his faint blush. She knew the sixteen-year-old had a crush on her, and she couldn't find it amusing, remembering her own first crush on a high-school teacher. It was kind of flattering too.

He hurried over and taped one of the fliers prominently in each of the front windows, then turned for her approval, beaming.

"That should help a lot, Steve. Thanks a million." She waved and turned to leave.

"Uh, Jamie, do you need any help on your place?" Steve's voice stopped her. "I'm strong—I haul bags of feed around all the time. I could do some of the heavy work for you."

Jamie swallowed. Oh, there was many a time when she could use a strong back and a pair of arms, even though Matt helped more than she should let him. "I'm sorry, Steve, but right now I can't afford to hire any help. I wish I could." She wondered at his wanting more work. She'd have thought he got enough of it helping his father in the store.

"I wouldn't expect you to pay me," Steve blurted. At Jamie's startled look, he went on, "I mean, what I want to do is ride horses, and I'd work in exchange for riding lessons and a chance to ride when I wanted to."

"Oh!" Jamie blinked, staring back at him, considering. "Why, sure, you could do that, Steve. But I think I'd be getting the best of the deal."

Steve grinned ear to ear. He shook his head earnestly. "No, you wouldn't. As soon as the store does better, Dad's going to buy some land out here and get some horses—but, shoot, by that time I'll be away in college! I want to ride now."

Jamie grinned back. "All right, you've got yourself a deal. When do you want to start?"

"How about tomorrow?" he asked eagerly. "Would that be too soon?"

Jamie laughed. "Nope. You just come over when you have some free time, and I'll always have something for you to do." For the next five years that would probably be true, she thought ruefully, as she waved and left the store.

She hadn't expected Steve's offer, but it was welcome. Now she wouldn't have to accept Matt's help all the time. He seemed to know when she was getting ready to do some hard job, and there he would be, "Just dropping by," he always said casually. He'd sit with her and Elinor and have iced tea or coffee. Then, just as casually, he'd find out what she planned to do that day, and somehow or other it always happened that he had a few free hours.

She appreciated the help—it saved her enormous amounts of time. For some of the work she would have had to hire help too, further

## Love's Gentle Season 33

depleting her rapidly dwindling savings. Sometimes she lay awake nights worrying, wondering if she'd made a mistake in buying the farm. Maybe she should have worked for another few years and saved more money.

*No!* she always answered herself after one of those late-night sessions. Another chance like this wouldn't come again. She'd been right to grab it. But suppose her parents were right? Suppose she failed? Then what? She turned those thoughts off fast, but still, in the deepest part of her mind, she was aware of them.

Now, the middle of July, a month after she'd moved here, the weather was hotter than ever. At least she wouldn't have to worry about her family visiting her now. And maybe by the time cool weather arrived, she'd have the place fixed up enough so that they'd be impressed with her ability and her business sense.

Fortunately, along with the heat there had been plenty of rain, so that the fertilizer she'd scattered soon after she arrived had made the grass turn a lush, deep green.

The next big job she had to tackle was repairing the fences in the lower pastures and putting in a lot of new posts and wire. If she got some horses to board, she'd need more grazing land. She didn't expect many boarders at first, but she still had to be prepared. Steve would be a big help. As he'd said, he was strong and used to hard physical work.

And she wouldn't let Matt know she was planning to start, or he'd be right there to help her. She couldn't keep on accepting his help and giving him nothing in return. He said he didn't mind and that that was what neighbors were for, but Jamie still felt that there was a limit.

Jamie slid behind the wheel of the pickup, gasping a little at the contact with the blistering-hot seat. She'd miss Matt's company, though, she had to admit. Easygoing and casual, his sense of humor exactly matched hers. Sometimes she wondered how Matt had been so successful at horse ranching, with his attitude.

But she really knew why. His surface manner was deceptive. Underneath the easygoing geniality, Matt was smart, savvy, and strong—he could handle anything he set his mind to, she figured.

He was also, she had to admit, the most attractive, completely masculine man she'd ever known. Just being around him when they were working together made her heart beat faster, and she was constantly aware of him as a man, not just a friend.

She didn't know how Matt felt. He certainly

## Love's Gentle Season

didn't seem to have any resentment toward her because she'd bought the farm. Usually he acted as if she were his sister, grinning at her, teasing her. Well, that was fine. She wasn't yet ready for anything serious with a man. She was too busy—and, besides, she had to be absolutely sure she could trust a man before she'd let one affect her emotions. Ted had cured her of getting involved too fast. Never again would she do that.

And she had no reason to think Matt was interested in her as anything but a friend. Except that a few times she'd caught him looking at her in a different way—as if he found her an attractive woman. He hadn't said anything, though, or acted any different. Maybe he, too, had had a bad relationship and was in no hurry to get involved again. Whatever the case, she was glad he wasn't trying to rush her into anything.

*But just the same, you wouldn't mind if he asked you for a date, would you?* That thought popped into her mind so unexpectedly that she jumped into the truck seat, trying to push it down. But once there, it stuck with her. No, she wouldn't mind if Matt asked her out—she wouldn't mind at all, she had to admit.

## Chapter Four

"Hard at it, I see."

Jamie's pulse leaped. She knew who that voice belonged to before she glanced up, pushing her sweat-dampened hair back. Matt stood a few feet away, giving her his easy smile, but his voice had sounded slightly stiff. She knew he wondered why she hadn't told him she was starting work on the fences today. After all, he'd offered to help several times.

"Hi, Matt." She returned his smile, hoping her own voice didn't register her discomfort. "Yes, we thought it was going to be cooler today. But I guess we were wrong."

She turned to include Steve Owens, standing beside her. Steve, his brow furrowed with concentration, was plunging a hand post-hole digger up and down in the sandy soil of the field.

The teenager glanced up. "Hi, Matt," he said, echoing Jamie's greeting. "Hot enough for you?"

"Sure is. You two are asking for heatstroke, working like that in this heat."

*Love's Gentle Season* 37

Now Jamie knew she hadn't been mistaken about the disapproval in Matt's voice. It came through loud and clear. She bit her lip, not knowing what to answer. Matt had offered more than once to dig the fence-post holes with the attachment on his tractor.

Steve shrugged manfully. "I've worked in hotter weather than this." It was obvious he felt some hero worship for Matt.

"So have I, but it's foolish to do this kind of work the hard way. How about if I bring the post-hole digger over?"

"Hey, that would be great!" Steve's brown eyes brightened. "We could get it done a lot faster."

Jamie looked from Steve to Matt. There was no way she could refuse Matt's help now, without sounding rude and ungrateful. "If you're not busy today, why, sure, that would help a lot."

Matt's blue eyes probed hers, as if trying to decide how she really felt. He shook his dark head. "No, I'm not busy today. I'll be back with the tractor in a few minutes." He turned and walked toward the house.

Steve's eyes followed him. "Boy, he sure knows a lot about horses," he told Jamie, turning toward her, his eyes shining. "My dad says when we do buy some, he's going to have Matt check them out for him first."

Relieved, Jamie saw he hadn't noticed any of the undercurrents between Matt and her. She smiled at him. "Yes, he does," she answered. "Well, since Matt is bringing the tractor over, what do you say we take a break until he gets back? We've been at it for over two hours."

Steve gave her a quick look, then put down the post-hole digger. "All right." He followed her to the shade of a live oak in the corner of the field, where they'd left a jug of ice water.

Jamie knew he didn't want her to think he was lazy, someone who jumped at a chance to quit working. He'd been helping her for two weeks now, and she'd never been sorry she'd taken him up on his offer. He was a hard worker, eager and willing. She sat down on the old blanket she'd also brought, checking first to see that there were no fire ants on it.

"How did Dusty do this morning?" she asked, uncapping the insulated jug and pouring a glass of water, which she handed to Steve. Steve was a natural rider, and by now she was letting him take Dusty out by himself.

He took a long drink before he answered. "Oh, he's great, Jamie. He makes me feel as

*Love's Gentle Season* 39

if I really know what I'm doing when I know I don't." He grinned at her.

Jamie laughed, understanding his slightly garbled sentence perfectly. Dusty was so responsive, so easy to control, he was ideal for new riders to learn on. Her fliers in the feed store had already attracted two other people for lessons—a sister and a brother. She'd had several calls about boarding, and one horse was supposed to come in this week. Things were picking up.

She heard the faint rumble of a tractor engine, and knew that Matt would soon be here. Well, she'd tried, and it hadn't worked. When did he ever get his own work done, she fretted, still uncomfortable with the situation.

The rumble grew louder, and soon the tractor appeared at the front gate. While Steve ran to open it for Matt, Jamie recapped the water jug and folded the blanket. She ran her fingers through her hair, wishing she'd brought along a comb. What did it matter, she asked herself impatiently; they were all going to be doing hard work in the hot sun. It was silly to care how she looked. She did, though.

The post-hole digger, which looked a bit like a giant corkscrew, was so much faster than working by hand that by twelve-thirty they were ready to string the wire.

"I don't know about you, but I need some nourishment." Matt pushed his straw hat back on his head.

"Me too," Steve agreed, moving his own hat back.

As if on cue, Elinor's voice called, "Come on, lunch is ready."

Jamie felt a pleasant sense of accomplishment as she walked back up the field between Steve and Matt. She'd been foolishly stubborn to resist Matt's offer of help. Especially this time, since she'd known, from her years on the horse farm, just how much time and work the machine could save. But she still felt bad about not returning the favors. If she could just think of something she could do for Matt. . . .

Then her steps slowed as an idea hit her. She'd been taking cooking lessons from her grandmother, and Elinor had pronounced her a natural good cook. Maybe Jamie could bake Matt some pies or a cake or two. What were his favorites?

"Hey, slowpoke, come on. We're starving."

Matt's teasing voice brought her out of her reverie, and she saw she'd fallen behind the other two. She hurried to catch up, trying to remember what he seemed to like best when he sampled Elinor's baking.

"Lemon meringue!" she said aloud, and

grinned as the two males stared at her. "I was just wondering if Gram had been doing any baking this morning," she hastily added.

"Gee, I hope so," Steve said. "Lemon pie is one of my favorites."

"Mine too," Matt said, still looking at Jamie.

It was one of those looks he gave her now and then, the kind that made her breathing quicken. But he'd confirmed her guess. She'd practiced on lemon-meringue pie until she had it down pat, the filling creamy and the topping light and fluffy every time.

"If you three aren't a pretty sight!" Elinor met them on the back porch. "Just head on back to the bathroom and wash off some of that dirt."

"You two go first." Jamie gave Matt and Steve a quick smile, then sat down on the porch swing, thinking over her new plan.

Elinor shook her head, sitting down beside her. "Jamie, I don't understand you sometimes. You go at everything like killing snakes. Why on earth didn't you let Matt use that machine in the first place?"

Jamie shrugged. She didn't want to get in an argument with her grandmother now. "I didn't want to keep on accepting favors from him without returning anything, Gram." She also didn't want to have Matt around so often either, because of the way he made her feel, but she wasn't going to tell Elinor that.

"I can understand that. But maybe he'll need something from us one of these days. He knows he can count on us anytime."

"Of course he can, but I just thought of something else." She glanced toward the kitchen to be sure Matt wasn't returning yet. "What does Matt like in the way of desserts, Gram?"

Elinor gave her a surprised look, then a smile formed on her mouth. "He's got a real sweet tooth, honey. I don't know of anything much he doesn't like, but especially chocolate."

Jamie grinned back. "And lemon-meringue pie."

Her grandmother nodded. "Yes, he loves that, and banana cream too." Male voices could be heard approaching. "Good thing Matt doesn't put on weight easy," she said quickly, just as Steve opened the screen, and came out, followed by Matt.

Jamie's eyes crinkled with suppressed laughter. "Yes, isn't it? I'm going to have to double up on my lessons." She grinned at Matt and Steve before going inside to take her turn at washing up.

Matt stared after her, then looked at Elinor. "What was that all about? Don't tell me Jamie is going to tackle something else."

Elinor gave a snort of laughter. "You might say so. Don't worry, Matt, you'll find out soon enough."

## Chapter Five

The next afternoon Jamie braked her truck in front of Matt's impressive house. She saw his Jeep out back, so he must be home. She reached for the basket on the seat beside her and, holding it carefully upright, walked up the flagstone walk and steps to the front door.

Instead of a bell, there was a brass knocker. She lifted it and let it fall, wincing at the loud noise it made. She tugged down her red T-shirt over her fresh jeans, feeling a little nervous. As often as Matt had been at her place, she hadn't been back here since the day she'd bought Misty. And she hadn't gone inside the house that day. What would he think of the offerings she carried in the basket?

After her first burst of enthusiasm, she'd gotten cold feet. Would he think she was trying to become too friendly with him by bringing him food? But her grandmother had urged her to act on the idea, and so she had. Inside the basket lay two of her best efforts: a lusciously creamy lemon pie, with high-piled meringue, and a pan of sinfully rich brownies.

She heard footsteps approaching the door. Her mouth suddenly felt dry, and her palms sweaty. She licked her lips; then the door swung open, and Matt stood there. He, too, wore jeans and T-shirt, and as usual, looked wonderful.

He gave her a surprised look, which quickly changed to a pleased smile. "Jamie! Come on in." He stepped back to let her enter the house.

Jamie smiled back, hoping she didn't look as nervous as she felt. Trying to hold the basket inconspicuously, she walked into the entryway. She sucked in her breath—oh, it was beautiful! The wide, white-tiled foyer led into a huge, open living room, with a stone fireplace going all the way up to the vaulted ceiling. A large skylight made the room bright and welcoming.

"Why are you holding that basket as if you didn't want me to see it?" Matt asked teasingly, as he led her to a long oatmeal-colored sofa. "Don't tell me you're bringing me a basket of kittens. I'm afraid Sheba won't like that."

As if to prove his point, a large white cat jumped down from a chair and moved majestically across the room, stopping in front of Jamie. She sat up on her haunches and regarded Jamie with unblinking green eyes.

Jamie hastily shook her head, setting the basket beside her. "You or Sheba don't have to worry about that. Her name certainly fits her," she added, feeling more uneasy about her plan by the second.

"Yes, she can be queenly enough when she wants to, which is most of the time." Matt sat down across from her on a matching chair. "If it's not kittens, what *is* in the basket?"

Jamie swallowed. Here in his house, Matt's strong masculine presence seemed to be affecting her more than it ever had. She wished that she hadn't brought the goodies, that she hadn't come. He probably would misunderstand, read more into the gesture than she intended. "Oh, this?" she said offhandedly. "It's just something I thought you might like."

Matt raised his dark brows. "A present for me? What did I do to deserve that?"

Jamie decided she was acting ridiculous, and she'd stop right now. "You've done all kinds of things for me," she said firmly, picking up the basket and extending it to Matt. "Here. Since you never seem to need any help with work, this was the only way to thank you I could think of."

Matt took the basket, lifted the hinged lid, and looked inside. His brows raised even higher, and he glanced at Jamie with a warm smile. "I take it the cooking lessons are working. These look wonderful."

Jamie shrugged, feeling her face reddening. How had he known that? "I hope so. Gram's a great teacher."

He stood up, holding the basket. "I know one thing. I'm not going to wait to sample them. I was going to offer you something to drink anyway. Iced tea all right?"

"Sure, fine," she answered. Just then Sheba leaped onto the sofa, and from there onto Jamie's lap, where she settled down and began purring loudly.

Matt paused halfway to the kitchen. "You should feel flattered. She doesn't like very many people. She must know you're a cat person."

Was she a cat person, Jamie wondered, reaching out a tentative hand to stroke down Sheba's silky back. She'd never had a cat—or a dog either, for that matter. Her parents thought animals were dirty and too much bother. Instead, they had a tank of brilliantly colored tropical fish.

The cat's back felt warm and alive, and she arched it at Jamie's touch, her purring increasing in volume. "She feels good!" Jamie said, her voice surprised.

Matt laughed. "Yes, she does. You sound as though you've never stroked a cat before."

Jamie raised her eyes to his. "Of course I have, but not lately."

"Good therapy," Matt said, his eyes twinkling. "When you're feeling down, there's nothing like a purring cat in your lap to cheer you up."

"I'd take you for a dog person," she answered, stroking the cat again.

"I am, but Bandit is at the ranch in Ocala. I'm gone so much here, I decided not to bring him. Dogs can't take too much of staying alone, the way cats can. My housekeeper feeds Sheba when I'm gone, and gives her some company while she's here during the day. I'll be right back. Do you want some pie or a brownie?"

Jamie quickly shook her head. "No, I had my fill while I was baking. Just tea, please."

"One glass of tea coming right up." Matt disappeared through a doorway across the big room. Jamie heard the refrigerator door open, then close, and the clatter of dishes and utensils.

She breathed a sigh of relief. Thank goodness that was over. And Matt didn't seem to think it was odd of her to bring him the goodies. She looked around the attractive room

## Love's Gentle Season 49

while she waited for him to come back. Matt had good taste in decorating, she decided, that is, if he'd made the decisions.

For all she knew, he'd hired a decorator. Or maybe someone in his family had helped. The room was a blend of earth tones, with bright gold and yellow and orange accents. The sofa she sat on was very comfortable, and the rest of the furniture looked as if it would be too. An antique gun collection occupied a corner cabinet.

The fireplace looked well used. The Panhandle had enough cold winter weather to make it welcome. Rows of bookshelves lined it on either side, holding volumes appearing equally well used. It was a room she instinctively liked and felt at home in.

"Here you are." Matt placed a glass of tea on the glass-topped table in front of her. He sat down across from her in the chair he'd occupied before, placing his own glass of tea across the table from hers. He held a plate with a generous piece of pie and two brownies on it. While Jamie watched, he took a forkful of pie and rolled his eyes in delight.

She smiled in relief. She'd been sure the brownies were good, because she'd tried one. She hadn't been able to do that with the pie, even though she'd been fairly certain it must taste all right. But it was good to know for sure. She picked up her glass of tea and sipped it.

"If you ever want to quit the horse business and go into baking, you won't lack for customers," he told her approvingly. "So this is the reward I get for helping you a few times?"

"It was more than a few times," Jamie said. "You've helped on almost every job I've done. I wouldn't have the stables operating this soon, if you hadn't given me so much help. I really appreciate it—but I don't like not being able to do anything for you in return. So—that's why—" She shrugged.

"You don't like to feel obligated, do you?" Matt asked her quietly. "I don't want you to feel like that with me, Jamie. I help you because I want to."

Jamie shrugged uneasily. "I know you do. And I guess you're right—I don't like to feel obligated. My family's given me so much hassle I suppose I feel I have to do this all by myself to prove I can." Now that she'd put it into words, she realized how true it was. It presented a picture of herself she didn't like. Did she really have that much of a chip on her shoulder?

"We all need other people. It's good to help each other. It's hard to go it alone." Matt was steadily working his way through the pie and the brownies.

"I know. And I don't really feel that way about other things. It's just this stable business."

"It must be rough to have your family disapprove of the way you want to live your life." Matt put the empty plate down on the coffee table and gave her a serious look, all his teasing gone. "I've always been lucky in that. My family loves the ranch. They visit every chance they get."

"Do you have brothers and sisters?" Jamie asked, realizing she knew very little about Matt's family.

He nodded. "One sister, Margaret, and a brother, Brad. They both live in Orlando, and so does my mother. She's been widowed for ten years."

Sheba suddenly decided she'd had enough of Jamie's lap and leaped down. She padded over to the wide window ledge and jumped up. Jamie saw she was intent on a mocking bird outside the window in the branches of a magnolia.

"I'm lucky to still have both my parents, I know," Jamie said. "I just wish we could be closer. If they could only realize I'm a grown woman and can run my life successfully." She sighed. "Sometimes I don't think they ever will."

"Sure they will. Just give them some more time. They can't help but be impressed with what you're doing here."

Jamie gave him a wry smile. "You don't know them. It takes a lot to impress my family. They're high achievers, all three of them." But she couldn't help feeling warmed and encouraged by his praise.

"You just don't have enough confidence in yourself," he said. He got up from his chair and sat down on the sofa beside her.

Why had he done that? Jamie kept her smile, but moved back a little. She shrugged. "Maybe I don't. I've always thought I did, since everything I've been doing for the last three years has been against my family's approval. But maybe I've been living on nerves."

Matt gave her his slow smile, and reached for her hand on the sofa beside her. "You're going to do fine. Just give yourself some time too." He enclosed her hand in his warm, strong one.

Tremors ran up and down Jamie's spine at his touch. His hand felt so good, so right somehow, holding hers. She hadn't expected him to do this, but now that he had, she was glad. She warmed her smile, leaving her hand enclosed

## Love's Gentle Season 53

in his. "I guess you're right. Now that I'm finally started on my dream, I get impatient. I want everything, including my family's approval, right now."

Matt's smile faded, and that look came over his face, the one that made her wonder how he really felt about her. His other hand moved up, brushing across her cheek lightly. "If it's any help, *I* thoroughly approve of you," he said softly. His eyes found her own.

Jamie felt her pulse racing at his touch, his words. She gazed into the blue depths of his eyes for a long moment, not wanting to break the spell that seemed to hold them.

"Jamie." Matt's words were a sigh as he leaned forward and gently pressed his lips to hers, his arm going around her shoulders to draw her closer to him.

She sucked in her breath, but she didn't draw away. She didn't even think about it. It felt too wonderful to be held in Matt's arms like this, to be kissing him.

In a moment, Matt moved back from her. "I've been wanting to do that ever since I saw you that first day out in the barn." The intent expression on his face slowly faded, and he smiled at her again.

Jamie smiled back, a little tremulously. She didn't know how to answer him. Anything she thought of sounded wrong. Finally, she stood up. "I guess I'd better go. I'm giving a riding lesson at five."

Matt stood too. His expression didn't change at her almost-abrupt words. He seemed to understand how she felt. "I'll get your basket." He went to the kitchen, and in a moment he returned with the wicker basket. "I'll carry it out to the truck for you."

"Oh, you don't have to bother," Jamie protested, then at once was sorry. It sounded as if she didn't want any more of Matt's company. Nothing could be further from the truth.

"No bother," he assured her, following as she walked toward the front door. Once there, he opened it for her, then closed it behind them.

The blast-furnace heat of a Florida late-July afternoon hit Jamie full force, almost taking her breath away. Matt's central air-conditioning had made her forget how hot it was. She was glad the lesson wasn't until five. It might be a little cooler by then.

Matt reached the truck before she did, and opened the door for her. "Thanks," she told him, sliding inside, glad the truck had been parked in the shade. "Good-bye, Matt. I—it was nice seeing you." *How awkward that sounded!* she berated herself. *Nice* wasn't how she'd describe what had just happened between them.

Matt leaned on the open window ledge. "Good-bye, Jamie. Thanks again for the goodies. You didn't have to do that."

She shook her head. "Oh, yes, I did. I'm not just a taker, I have to give too." Her feelings were mixed up about the fact that Matt was apparently going to ignore what had happened between them. She was glad he wasn't going to make a big deal out of a kiss, but on the other hand, she'd like to think that it meant something to him, as well as to her.

"I know you do." Matt's voice had softened again, as it had a few minutes ago when he'd told her he'd wanted to kiss her ever since that first day. "Look, you know the old saying about all work and no play? Would you like to take in a movie some night soon?"

Jamie stared at him in surprise for a moment. Then she gave him a straight, clear look. "That sounds like fun."

"Good. How about Saturday night? There's a comedy playing downtown in Pensacola that's supposed to be good."

"All right. What time?" She was glad her voice sounded so easy.

"How about the early one—seven-thirty? We could eat somewhere first."

She nodded. "Fine. I haven't seen a movie all summer."

"Okay, it's all set, then. I'll pick you up about six."

"I'll be ready."

Matt took his arms off the window ledge, and moved back from the truck. Jamie twisted the key in the ignition and gave him a wave as she turned the truck.

She felt elation filling her as she drove down the long lane back toward the county road. She'd wanted Matt to ask her out, and he had. As for the kiss—had she wanted that too? She didn't know, but it had been pleasant, anyway.

"Let's be honest about this, Jamie," she said aloud, pausing to look both ways before pulling out into the road. "It was a lot more than pleasant, and you know it."

## *Chapter Six*

"**G**ram, do you think this looks all right?" Jamie anxiously smoothed the skirt of her pale yellow summer dress as she waited for Matt to pick her up.

"Oh, for heaven's sake, stop fussing!" Elinor exclaimed. "No one dresses up around here, unless they're going to a funeral or a wedding."

Jamie let out a sigh. "You're right. It's just that I've lived in jeans all summer. I hardly know how to dress any other way."

"You look fine. Matt will think so too," Elinor said dryly. "You're acting as if you've never had a date before."

Jamie grinned. "Well, that's about how I feel. I haven't dated much since Ted and I broke up. I didn't really want to before."

"But now you do." Elinor picked up her knitting basket and started working on a red sweater.

"Well, yes," Jamie answered slowly, plucking a tiny piece of lint off the dress. She didn't look her grandmother in the eye.

"I can understand that. If I were young today, I'd call Matt a hunk."

Jamie laughed out loud. She knew her grandmother too well to be surprised at anything she might say. "I guess so," she agreed. "But he's a lot more than that."

"Sure he is. If I were thirty years younger, I'd go after him myself." She looked up at Jamie, her dark eyes twinkling.

Jamie frowned. "I'm not 'going after Matt,' Gram. We're just going to a movie. We may never date each other again."

"Ha! Tell me something I'll believe. You and Matt are suited to a T."

Jamie felt her face reddening, and she turned away to stare out the window. "I've known him only a few weeks," she protested. She wasn't ready yet to talk like this, even to think like this. And she was sure Matt wasn't either.

"Your grandfather and I knew how we felt the first time we saw each other." Elinor's words were calm and sure.

Jamie felt relieved when she heard a vehicle stop outside. This conversation was getting out of hand. She was glad Matt had come and she could leave. She glanced out to see an unfamiliar black sports car and frowned. Who was that? Then, to her surprise, Matt opened the

## Love's Gentle Season 59

door, got out, and began walking toward the house.

"There's Matt, Gram." Her voice contained a slight warning note.

"All right, I can take a hint," Elinor said comfortably. "I'm not going to put my foot in my mouth."

"Good." Jamie opened the door to Matt's knock. He wore well-fitting gray slacks and a blue sports shirt, she saw, relieved that she looked all right. He was about as dressed up as she was.

"Hi, come on in," she said, stepping back to let him enter.

Matt's eyes swept over her, and then his slow smile lit his tanned face as he walked inside. "I hardly recognized you in a dress. You should wear one more often."

"I'll try it next time I'm mucking out the stalls." Jamie smiled back, but she felt her pulse fluttering. Matt's glance had been full of flattering admiration, and she didn't know how to deal with it. *Since you've already been kissed by him, an admiring glance shouldn't throw you,* she told herself derisively.

"Hello, Elinor," Matt greeted the older woman. "Sure you won't change your mind and come with us?" His voice was teasing.

Elinor put her knitting down in her lap and

regarded Matt with approval. "You'd be in a pretty pickle if I took you up on that, wouldn't you?" She grinned at him. "You look plenty sharp yourself, Matt."

Matt shrugged. "Feels funny to be out of jeans. The only time I wear suits anymore is on my business trips."

He felt a little embarrassed too, Jamie saw, and wondered why. Did he think her grandmother was reading more into the date than it warranted? She felt her face reddening again. Even if her grandmother didn't say anything, her attitude couldn't help but show. "I guess we'd better go if we want to eat before the movie," she said quickly.

Matt glanced at her curiously. "All right, let's go," he answered, turning back toward the door. "Good night, Elinor."

"Good night, you two. Have fun."

Jamie felt her face redden even more as she followed Matt out to his car. Now he probably thought she was in a big hurry to be alone with him. Even with the bucket seats, they seemed to be sitting too close together, Jamie thought, resisting an urge to move closer to the door.

What on earth was wrong with her tonight? Not only was she acting as if this was her first date, as her grandmother had said, she was also behaving as if Matt was a stranger, instead of

## Love's Gentle Season 61

a man she'd been working closely with for weeks now, and had become good friends with.

And that was exactly what was wrong, she suddenly saw. Ever since she'd taken Matt the baked goodies a few days ago and he'd kissed her, she hadn't seen him. He'd gone off to Ocala on one of his business trips, and had just gotten back today. She guessed she wasn't sure how to handle their being together now. Could they just be friends, or would things be different? And did she want them to be different?

"Where would you like to eat?" Matt asked, breaking the silence. "A steak house, or someplace a little fancier?" His voice sounded easy and friendly, just as it always did.

Jamie let out a relieved breath. "I don't care, anywhere you like. I haven't eaten out since I've been here. I don't know anything about the restaurants."

"All right—let's make it a steak house tonight, since we don't have a whole lot of time. There are a couple of nice restaurants we can try some other time."

He hadn't been put off by her grandmother, then. He intended to ask her out again. Jamie's relief grew, making her see she'd just answered her own question. Yes, she did want this new relationship with Matt to grow. She wanted to be more than friends.

* * *

The food was good, and the movie hilarious. They talked easily, as they always had, but there seemed to be some new kind of undercurrent to their words and glances. Jamie enjoyed the evening hugely, and was sorry to see it end. "You were right about all work and no play making a person dull," she told Matt on the way home. "I've had a great time."

"Good." Matt's voice was approving as he skillfully drove the car down the almost-deserted interstate. "Now I know I can ask you out again, and maybe you won't say no."

Jamie felt some of her tense wariness return. What was Matt really saying? That he wanted to enjoy more casual dates, or that he wanted them to become closer than friends? "I'd like to go out with you again," she finally answered.

The mood between them seemed to have changed again, she realized. The easy companionship had given way to a kind of tense expectancy in the close confines of the small car. They didn't say much the rest of the way home. Matt finally pulled up in the driveway before the darkened house and switched off the engine.

Jamie turned to him, smiling a little stiffly. "Thanks for a nice evening, Matt, I'd better—"

Her words died away as she saw the intent expression on his face.

"Jamie. . . ." Matt leaned across the seat and reached for her. "You're so lovely. . . ."

As if in a dream, Jamie moved closer, lifting her face to his, and Matt's lips came down on hers. This kiss was different from the first one, more intense. Matt's hand on her back pressed her closer to him, and she thrilled to his closeness.

At last he ended the kiss, and Jamie moved back in her seat, shaken by the way it had made her feel. She smoothed her tumbled hair back from her flushed face.

"Well, I guess I'd better go in. Tomorrow's going to be. . . ." Her voice trailed off again. She'd started to say how busy she'd be, but tomorrow was Sunday. She'd go to church with Elinor in the morning, then spend the afternoon resting or cooking or catching up on things she'd let slide.

"Yes, I suppose I should get some sleep too. I may have to go back to Ocala tomorrow night." Matt's voice sounded completely normal and ordinary now.

Jamie pressed her lips together in embarrassment. Obviously the kiss hadn't meant as much to Matt as it had to her. Why was she worrying about things going too fast between them? She opened the car door and got out before Matt could come around, and even though he walked her to the door, he didn't kiss her again. He just gave her a friendly wave, as he always did.

"See you in a few days, Jamie." He smiled and left, making no mention of another date.

Jamie closed and locked the door, and went quietly to her room, glad her grandmother hadn't waited up for her. She didn't feel like any rehashes of the evening. The evening had been wonderful, except for the end of it.

No, that wasn't true, she admitted to herself, Matt's kiss still tingling on her lips. The problem was her own confused feelings, and not knowing how Matt really felt. On the one hand, she wanted to become closer to Matt, to be more than friends; yet another part of her told her to be wary and cautious, not to trust too soon.

As she had with Ted. She'd eagerly accepted Ted's whirlwind courtship with no doubts at all, even accepted his engagement ring. Then had come the shattering discovery that without the prospect of her having a professional career, without the prestige of her family's law firm behind her, Ted hadn't wanted her.

But that had nothing to do with this relationship with Matt, she told herself firmly.

Matt had nothing to gain by romancing her. Then she stopped dead just inside her bedroom door, a cold feeling moving down her spine.

Or did he? He hadn't said anything lately about trying to buy the acreage to the west. He hadn't mentioned it at all. And he loved the old farm she'd bought from her grandmother; she could see that. Maybe that was why he came over so often.

Maybe that was why he had asked her out. Maybe that was why he'd kissed her. Maybe he'd decided that if he couldn't buy the land, he could acquire it in another way.

Feeling numb and sick, Jamie got ready for bed. Matt wasn't that kind of person. He was honest and caring. He wouldn't do something like that. But no matter how she tried to convince herself, another thought kept intruding.

She hadn't thought Ted was that kind of person, either. But she'd been wrong.

## Chapter Seven

"Good morning, Jamie." Neal Gardner, the rural mail carrier, smiled as he handed her a stack of envelopes. "Looks like rain. We could use some."

Jamie returned his smile as she took the stack, which seemed to be mostly bills and junk mail. "Yes, we could. This sandy soil dries out in a hurry."

"I hear you're giving riding lessons now."

Jamie nodded. "Yes, I started several weeks ago. If you know of anyone who's interested, let me know."

Neal hesitated a moment before he spoke. "Our daughter, Lori, would love to learn to ride, but I don't guess that's possible, because she's handicapped."

"In what way, Neal?" Jamie asked carefully. "I worked with handicapped children on the horse farm, and lots of them can learn to ride."

Neal's pleasant face looked surprised, then brightened with interest. "I didn't know that.

## Love's Gentle Season 67

I'd thought it would take someone with full control."

Jamie shook her head. "No, I worked with a therapeutic riding group. They trained horses and volunteers to help with all kinds of handicaps—emotional as well as physical. Is Lori physically handicapped?"

He nodded. "She's deaf. She goes to a special school and is learning to talk, but it's slow going. She resists because signing is so much easier for her."

Jamie nodded in understanding. "I worked with a deaf child. Davey's speech improved a good bit. Handicapped children usually try harder, so that gives them a boost to start with. How old is Lori?"

"Ten," Neal answered. "She was born deaf, so she doesn't know how speech should sound. Do you really think this would work for her?"

Jamie abruptly realized what she was saying. She'd encouraged Neal, when she had no horses or facilities to help him with his daughter. But maybe there was a way. "Yes, I do, Neal, but I don't have any trained horses here."

His face fell in disappointment. "I should have realized that. Well, thanks, anyway." He waved and started to turn away.

"Wait, Neal," Jamie said quickly, moving

forward a step. "I wasn't finished. How about if I try to find out if there's an organization like that here? If so, I'll let you know, and you can get in touch with them."

He smiled at her warmly. "Thanks again, Jamie. But you don't have to bother. Maybe I can find out something."

"It wouldn't be a bother," Jamie said firmly. "I enjoyed working with the riding group; I'd like to do it again."

"All right, then, if you're sure." Neal waved again, then drove off.

Jamie stared after him thoughtfully, wondering if she'd been too impulsive. She was already putting in long, tiring days trying to turn her stables into a paying business. How could she squeeze in another job? Well, she just would, she decided, turning to go back to the house.

If there was a handicapped riding group here, she felt sure they'd need volunteers. She could still remember the look of proud achievement on a child's face after mastering some part of riding skills, and the warm glow it had given her. Somehow, she'd find time to help.

Jamie put down the phone, a frown on her face. She turned to her grandmother, who was pouring boiling water into a teapot. "I hate to

## Love's Gentle Season 69

tell Neal the bad news—there is a group here, but it's never gotten off the ground."

Elinor looked up. "Why not?"

"Lack of facilities, mostly. They have a few trained horses, but no place to give the riding instruction." Her voice held a question as she returned her grandmother's glance.

Elinor picked up on it at once. "What do they need?" She took down cups from a wall rack, and filled them with tea from the pot. She handed Jamie one, then sat down at the table.

Jamie absentmindedly took the cup, sitting down too. "Oh, nothing too elaborate. An arena of some kind, a small pasture. A lunge pen would help. And some kind of rest-room facilities."

"Are you thinking about volunteering your stables?"

As usual, her grandmother had gotten right to the point. Jamie looked at her, biting her lip. "I don't know. I've got so much to do anyway, I shouldn't get involved in anything else. But I know what this program can do for handicapped people. They told me they can bring in portable rest rooms. And there's the lunge pen we just built. So, I—"

"So you'll go ahead and do it, and find the time," Elinor finished, lifting her cup to her lips.

Jamie nodded. "Yes, I guess I will. You wouldn't mind, would you, Gram?"

Elinor shook her head vigorously. "Of course not. Besides, you seem to forget it's your place now to do with as you please."

Jamie grinned. "Maybe I do. All right, I'm going to do it." She got up again and walked over to the wall phone, taking her cup of tea with her. "I'll see what I can find out."

"Have you thought about asking Matt if he'd like to help with the program?" Elinor asked as Jamie dialed the number she'd been given a few minutes ago.

Jamie shook her head without turning around. "No, Gram. I've already accepted too much help from Matt. I couldn't ask him to do anything else."

"As far as I know, you've never asked him to do anything. He's always volunteered," Elinor answered crisply. "He might like to help with this."

Jamie shrugged, listening to the phone ring. "I know, but still—" She broke off as a voice answered at the other end. "Hello, is this Linda Wills? This is Jamie Richards. I have some stable facilities that might do for your handicapped riding program." She talked for a few minutes, then hung up and turned back to her grandmother, a satisfied smile on her face.

"Linda has a handicapped son—and she worked with a program like this before she moved here. She and a group of other people have been trying to organize one here for a year or so. She's coming out tomorrow to look over the stables to see if they will do."

Elinor smiled back as she got up from the table. "Good. But I still think you should tell Matt about it."

Jamie's smile turned into a half frown. She hadn't seen Matt for two weeks, not since their dinner and movie date. Matt had told her that night he'd be seeing her in a few days. He'd as much as said he wanted to go out with her again.

But he hadn't called, and he hadn't come over. "That might be hard to do, Gram, since I haven't seen him lately." The unhappy edge in her voice came through, even though she'd tried to keep her grandmother from knowing how she felt.

Elinor gave her granddaughter a keen glance. "Don't worry about him, Jamie. He's probably just been busy. I'm sure he'll be over in a day or so."

Jamie turned and walked briskly to the sink. "I'm not worried," she insisted. "What Matt Douglas does is no concern of mine." She washed the cups, and put them into the drainer.

Elinor emptied the teapot and handed it to Jamie. "Just as you say, honey," she said mildly. "Don't get your back up."

Jamie wiped off the countertop and put the sponge away, not looking at her grandmother. She knew if their eyes met, she wouldn't be able to keep up the fiction that Matt's continued absence didn't bother her. In spite of what she'd told herself that night after their date, in spite of her uneasiness about Matt's possible motives in taking her out, in kissing her, the fact remained that she missed him more than she wanted to admit.

Jamie reined Misty in as they approached a large, irregular sunken place in the field, skirting it carefully. She'd have to fill that in this afternoon, she told herself, making a mental note. The soft, sandy Panhandle soil was prone to these sinkholes, and as Misty's foaling date drew closer and the mare grew more sleek and rounded every day, Jamie worried about her falling or otherwise injuring herself.

The sound of hoofbeats came from behind her, and Jamie half turned. Matt, mounted on his bay gelding, Toby, cantered toward her. Matt! She felt her heart leap, and a thrill of

## Love's Gentle Season 73

pleasure went through her. Another week had passed, and she still hadn't seen or heard from him—until now. "Whoa," she told Misty, tugging lightly on the reins. The obedient mare at once halted, standing quietly as Jamie waited for Matt to reach them.

"I see you're taking advantage of this weather too." He reined Toby in beside Jamie, his smile warm and friendly, no trace of anything else in it.

"Yes." Jamie's answering smile reflected the warmth of his, and how his presence was making her feel. "There aren't too many days like this in August here." A cold front had blown in with a rainfall during the night, leaving the morning crisp and almost cool—a feeling of coming autumn in its breeze.

"That's for sure," Matt agreed, "except for the thunderstorms. And we're due at least one hurricane scare before the season's over. Are you just starting your ride, or are you almost finished?"

"I was nearly ready to come in. I've been out about half an hour. I wanted to give Misty some exercise."

Matt gave the mare an appraising glance. "She's looking good," he said. "She should be foaling in another few weeks."

"I can't wait—but I'm a little nervous too."

Jamie gently touched Misty's sleek sides, and the mare began moving forward again.

"Nature usually takes care of these things just fine." Matt urged his mount ahead too, keeping up with Jamie.

Jamie felt a surge of elation filling her. It felt wonderful riding along with Matt in the crisp morning air. "I know, I saw quite a few foalings at the horse farm, but I keep thinking of all the things that could go wrong."

Matt gave her a quick glance, and their eyes met for a long moment. "Don't worry," he said reassuringly. "I'll be right next door if you should need me."

That look from his blue eyes unsettled her, reminding her of the last time they'd been together—and Matt's disturbing good-night kiss. "I can't really count on that, can I?" she asked, chagrined at hearing the edge in her voice. She hadn't wanted to let him know how she felt about his long absence.

"Oh, so you missed me, huh?" Matt's deep voice held a teasing note.

"No!" Jamie said quickly. "I mean, how long you stay away is your own business," she floundered, embarrassment sweeping over her.

"I had a lot of things to take care of," he answered, the teasing note gone now. "I have a

*Love's Gentle Season* 75

good manager, but some things Joe can't handle. I missed you, Jamie."

Jamie sucked in her breath, not sure how to reply, and wondering at that moment of hesitation in his voice when he talked about his ranch. Did he think she was prying? She darted another quick glance at Matt, to find him looking straight at her, his expression serious.

She felt herself reddening under his scrutiny. Should she admit she'd missed him too? More than she wanted to acknowledge? *Stop acting coy, Jamie Richards,* she admonished herself. *You're not that type, and you know it.* She took a deep breath, and turned toward him again, her eyes steady on his. "Yes, I missed you, Matt," she told him.

Matt's serious look slid into a grin. "Good! Then maybe you won't turn me down if I ask you to go out to dinner with me again."

She let her breath out in relief and grinned back, glad he was lightening the mood. She wasn't ready for anything heavy yet, and Matt was making it plain he wasn't either. "You could try," she suggested. They were approaching the fence at the far end of her property, and she tugged on the reins to turn Misty.

The horses in a smooth walk, they rode back toward the barn in a companionable silence. Matt was easy to be around, Jamie thought.

She felt no need to keep up a constant stream of conversation, no awkwardness when a silence fell, as now.

"How about Saturday evening?" Matt suddenly asked. "To go out, I mean. Maybe we could try a fancier place this time."

"All right," Jamie said, then stopped. "Oh, Matt, I can't, not this Saturday. The people from the handicapped riding group are bringing their horses in the late afternoon, and I need to stick around to see they settle in all right."

"Handicapped riding group?" Matt repeated, his voice puzzled.

"Yes—oh, I forgot you haven't been here since I got involved with them." She quickly explained to Matt about her conversation with Neal Gardner and how it had led to her inquiries about the organization.

"So now you're going to board some of their horses?" Matt asked, interest apparent in his voice.

She nodded. "Yes. Right now they have only three. Last week they brought them out in trailers, for the riding session, but that was such a hassle I told them I had room for them here. I'm also helping as a sidewalker, something I did when I worked at the horse farm."

"Sidewalker—is that what it sounds like, you walk alongside the horse?"

Jamie nodded again. "To steady the rider. There's one on each side when they start out." By now they'd reached the barn, and Jamie stopped Misty, then dismounted.

Matt was now standing beside Toby too. "Do they need any more volunteers? I could help with that."

Jamie looked at him in pleased surprise. Her grandmother had been right again. And she had no qualms about accepting his help this time because it wasn't for herself. "Are you kidding? They always need volunteers."

"Fine. When do they give the instruction?" Matt looped Toby's reins around a fence post.

"It will be Monday and Friday afternoons, starting at two. Would you like to come this afternoon and watch? You'll need some training before you can help, but that won't take long." She pulled off the pad she'd used in place of a saddle, then unfastened Misty's bridle and removed it. The morning was still cool, and Jamie hadn't ridden her hard, of course, so Misty wouldn't need walking or rubbing down. The mare moved away and began grazing in the small field.

"I'd like that. This sounds like a very worthwhile thing to do, Jamie." Matt gave her an admiring, approving look as he reached for the pad.

She gave it to him, feeling a warm glow. She hadn't told him to gain his approval, but it was nice, just the same. She followed him to the small tack shed, carrying the bridle. "At the horse farm I saw how much good it could do. Sometimes it almost seems to work miracles."

Matt laid the blanket across a sawhorse, while Jamie hung the bridle on a wall hook. They both straightened up at the same time. She was suddenly very conscious that they were alone in the small enclosure. It reminded her of those few minutes in his car the last time they'd been together. Her breath came faster as she smiled at him, remembering.

"Jamie—" Matt moved a step closer to her. "I have missed you a lot." His eyes seemed a more intense blue in the dimness of the shed.

Jamie remembered how she had felt when he'd kissed her. Was he going to kiss her now? Then, abruptly, another memory came into her mind: how she'd wondered, after she went into the house, if she was too trusting of Matt's motives, if his real interest was in her—or in her land.

With this thought, she instinctively stepped backward, toward the door.

Matt didn't follow her. He stopped where he

## Love's Gentle Season 79

was, his face serious as his eyes probed hers. Then, the serious look faded, replaced by a grin. He turned to push the saddle pad more securely onto the sawhorse. "If Saturday evening's out, how about Sunday?" he asked, facing her again.

Jamie felt confused. One minute Matt acted as if he wanted to kiss her, the next as if they were nothing more than casual friends. How did he really feel? She frowned as if trying to remember if she was busy Sunday night, though she knew she wasn't. Finally she nodded. "I'd like that. But, Matt, we don't have to go to a fancy place. The steak house is fine."

His grin widened. "Do you really mean that? Because I hate fancy places."

She nodded vigorously. "I do too." She walked through the doorway as he came toward her, stopping just outside.

"A woman after my own heart."

Matt's warm breath tickled her neck as his deep voice rumbled in her ear. That was an innocent phrase, but it could also hold a world of meaning. And what did Matt mean by it, anyway? He was an intriguing, puzzling man.

Another disturbing thought surfaced. No matter how she fought against admitting it, she was beginning to feel something much deeper than just attraction for Matt Douglas.

## Chapter Eight

"I can't believe that Lori's made so much improvement in such a short time." Lori's mother, Denise, a vivacious dark-haired woman, stood with Jamie as they watched a riding session.

Jamie's eyes followed Lori as she confidently walked the bay gelding around the arena, her blond braids bobbing under her safety helmet. "Yes, she certainly has. I've seen this happen before, but it's always such a satisfaction when it works."

"I can't thank you enough for getting us involved with this program, Jamie. It's changed Lori's whole life. All I *hear,*" she said, stressing the last word, "is horse, horse, horse—and I love it! All the verbal instruction has helped with her speech more than I'd have believed possible in only a few weeks." Denise flashed Jamie a warm smile.

"Just seeing her like this—and listening to her speak—is thanks enough," Jamie answered, returning the smile, her satisfaction turning into a warm glow.

"I know it takes a lot of your time, though, and you're working hard enough at starting your stables. We really appreciate it. If there's anything we can do to help you, let us know."

"Thanks," Jamie said, "but you and Neal are already helping a lot with the therapeutic riding program. Linda told me how good you and Neal are with the fund raising and the public-relations work you've been doing."

Denise shrugged. "We felt it was the least we could do after what it's done for Lori." Her eyes went to the other horse in the arena. "Matt is so good with the children, isn't he?"

Jamie followed her gaze, her breath quickening as she watched Matt lead the other horse, a black gelding. Danny Andrews sat astride him, carefully assisted on either side by Steve and his girlfriend, Carol. Danny's back was still painfully bent from the spinal curvature he'd had since birth, but already he sat straighter in the saddle, his manner a little more confident with each session.

"Yes, he is," she answered, her mouth involuntarily curving in a smile as she watched Matt work with confidence and ease. Matt had been recruited for a leader at once, since he was so knowledgeable about horses. Steve had been enthusiastic about helping as a sidewalker, and had brought Carol along for the first training session. They'd proved to be very dependable, and the children liked them because they were closer to their own age, and so cheerful and casual with them.

"I hear Matt's lawyer has taken over the legal work for the organization," Denise went on. "And Matt is paying for it, as well as furnishing transportation for some of the kids."

"Yes, that's true," Jamie acknowledged. So much had happened this last month it didn't seem possible it had been such a short time since it all started. "It really helps, because, as you know, our budget is awfully small." She smiled as she listened to the *our* slip out easily. She'd gotten more involved than she planned, but she hadn't regretted it for a second.

Denise sighed. "Don't I know it! It's so hard to get people interested in helping, what with all the other charities around. I try to explain that this isn't a charity, but something that can benefit the whole community by helping to make handicapped people more independent, but sometimes it just doesn't register."

"I guess it's because most people have never heard of a therapeutic riding program. After all, there are only a few programs like this in the whole country," Jamie said, her eyes still on Matt. His dark hair glinted in the afternoon sunshine, making a tingle go down her spine.

They'd gone out together several times in the last few weeks, since that second date, when he'd just gotten back from Ocala. And they had a date tonight too. Her heart beat faster at the thought of being alone with him in just a few more hours.

She didn't know where they were going—Matt had been very secretive about it, in a teasing kind of way. Her anticipation grew as she thought about it. Then she frowned. That is, if Matt didn't get a sudden call to return to Ocala. That had happened a couple of times this last month too. His business problems seemed to be increasing lately.

He must find it hard to run his big ranch from here, even if he did have an excellent business manager. She wondered uneasily if he had any plans to move back there. After all, he hadn't said anything about buying more land in this area lately.

She firmly pushed all these thoughts aside, and turned her attention back to the riding session. Lately, she'd been successful in doing that—especially when she and Matt were together. She enjoyed being with him so much, it was easy to forget there were unresolved questions floating around in the back of her mind.

A sudden gust of wind blew across the field, whirling a few scattered leaves and making Jamie grab for her cap.

Denise laughed as she, too, reached for her cap. "I hope that's not a sign old Edna is heading our way." She glanced at the partly overcast sky.

"So do I," Jamie answered. Edna wasn't the first tropical storm this season, but the others had all fizzled out before doing any damage. The weather forecasters were warning this one might be different. And even though still out in the Gulf of Mexico somewhere, and not posing a threat to this area yet, Edna could change course anytime.

The session over, Matt, Steve, and Carol led the gelding over to the dismounting ramp. They helped Danny off the horse, then he removed the safety helmet and handed it to Steve. He walked back with Steve and Carol as they led the horse toward the barn, where Jamie knew he'd insist on rubbing him down and brushing him. That was an important part of the training too, helping the children build self-confidence in their abilities.

Matt came over to where she and Denise stood by the fence. "Danny really did well today, didn't he?" His warm smile lit his face with satisfaction.

"He sure did!" Denise smiled back, then moved forward. "I see Lori is about finished; I'll go help her. I'll be seeing you two." She waved and walked toward her daughter, who was maneuvering her horse toward the dismounting ramp.

Matt looked tired. Jamie suspected he was losing some sleep trying to keep up with the demands of his two ranches and his involvement with the riding group. She gave him a rueful smile. "Are you ready to strangle me for getting you into all this?"

He shook his head emphatically. "Nope. It's a lot of work, but I don't know when I've done anything that was so rewarding. You can *see* the results of what you're trying to do with these kids."

Jamie nodded, relieved. "Yes, I know. It's exciting to see how quickly things can improve with them." She hesitated, then said, "Matt, if you're tired, we don't have to go anywhere tonight. I mean," she went on quickly, so he wouldn't think she was trying to get out of their date, "you can eat dinner with Gram and me if you'd rather." Jamie's cooking lessons had expanded to include entire meals, and Matt had eaten with them several times.

Matt grinned, then shook his head again. "Not on your life! I'm going to turn the tables on you tonight—you're going to have to sample some of my cooking for a change."

Jamie's anticipation returned full force. "I can't wait. I've been wondering if your housekeeper cooked too, or if you ate out of cans."

He gave her a mock-wounded look. "Just for that, I'll make you wash the dishes. Of course I can cook, even though Mrs. Collins leaves me a meal on the days she's here, I'll admit. I'm also a mean hand with a can opener. But tonight," he said, giving her an exaggerated, sweeping bow, "no cans, I promise you. Strictly Matt Douglas originals."

Jamie laughed. She loved his sense of humor, she loved so many things about him. She— Suddenly, her thoughts stopped dead as she realized what she'd been about to think.

She swallowed a sudden lump in her throat. "I'd better help get everything finished here, then, so you can go home and get started." A sudden thought struck her. "I can just drive over to your place, since we're eating there, and you won't have to come and get me," she suggested.

"All right," Matt agreed. "About six-thirty?"

"Fine. See you then." She waved and headed

toward the barn, hoping her expression hadn't given away her thoughts. As much fun as she and Matt had together, as close as she often felt to him, she didn't know any more about how he felt than she had the first day they'd met.

*So, my girl,* she admonished herself, *you'd just better cool it for a while, because you aren't at all sure how you feel, either, are you?*

"As you can see, I remembered you told me you didn't like fancy food." Matt deftly slid a thick, sizzling steak from the brick fireplace grill onto Jamie's plate and handed it to her with a flourish. "I don't cook fancy, but I do cook good." He grinned at her.

Jamie's hand brushed his as she took the plate and placed it on the red-checked tablecloth on the patio table. "You're also extremely modest." She grinned back at him, still feeling the touch of his warm hand. He'd changed from his work-stained jeans to dark blue slacks, his shirt a lighter blue. She was glad she'd decided to wear the mint-green sundress that brought out the green flecks in her eyes, and glad as well that she'd taken her hair down from its customary ponytail, brushing it over her shoulders.

"I'm pleased you noticed."

He put his own steak on another plate, and

Jamie took that one too, placing it across the table from hers. The evening was warm, but a breeze was coming up, gusting every now and then, reminding Jamie of Edna. The storm had been upgraded to hurricane strength, and it was still southwest of them in the Gulf.

Matt put foil-wrapped baked potatoes on their plates, then set a large bowl of green salad in the middle of the table. "Would you like some wine?" he asked.

Jamie felt a small moment of alarm. No, she didn't want any wine! She already felt half intoxicated just being with Matt; she didn't need anything else. Then she told herself she was being silly. "Yes, that would be nice," she answered.

In a moment he was back with a bottle of rosé and two wineglasses. He filled their glasses, then set the wine in an ice bucket he'd brought out, and sat down across from her. A sudden gust of wind rattled the screening of the enclosed patio where they sat, making Jamie glance up uneasily.

"This one may amount to something," Matt said. "It's been a couple of years since we've had any real hurricanes, so I guess it's about time for a good one." He lifted his glass to her.

Jamie returned the gesture, her uneasiness increasing. "Don't say that! No hurricane is 'good.' I've never lived this close to the coast before—could it really do a lot of damage here?"

Matt put down his glass and picked up his fork, giving her a reassuring smile. "Probably not. We're in a well-protected area—we have a lot of forest, with some big trees between us and the water. But when it comes to hurricanes, you never really know. They're so unpredictable."

"That really makes me feel a lot better." She put down her glass, her own smile wry. "Do we need to worry about the horses?"

"No, I don't think so," Matt said quickly. "Horses are pretty smart about storms. They'll instinctively go to the most protected area and stay there."

"Do you mean we shouldn't shut them in the barn?" she asked, looking at him in surprise.

Matt shook his head. "No, that would be more dangerous than leaving them in the open." At her look of alarm, he went on, "Don't worry, Jamie. It's still a long way off. It will probably come in farther west or dissipate."

"That's the horrible thing about hurricanes, you have to wish them on someone else, some other place, so you won't get them."

"I guess that's true," Matt conceded, "but let's forget about it for now."

"All right," she agreed, forking up a piece of the delectable-looking steak. "Ummm, this is wonderful! You've been holding out on me, Matt!"

He shrugged. "I don't like to brag about my accomplishments," he answered, grinning at her. "Especially when they turn out well. Steaks are the best thing I do," he admitted.

"I could live on these for a while." She dug into her meal with appreciation and an appetite whetted by a long day of rigorous physical labor.

They talked casually while they ate, and afterward Jamie insisted on helping clean up, even though Matt told her just to leave everything, his housekeeper was coming in the morning.

"She'd love to clean up this mess! No, we can do it in a few minutes." She briskly cleared the table, piling the dishes onto a tray and taking them into Matt's ultra-convenient kitchen. It was as modern as her own was old-fashioned, but somehow it, too, had a welcoming, homey feel to it.

Maybe it was because of the bright lemon-yellow walls, she decided, or the glowing wood tones of the fruit-wood cabinets. Whatever, it made her feel welcome at once. She heard a plaintive meow at her feet and glanced down to see Sheba sitting in front of her. The cat's eyes were riveted on the plate of steak scraps Jamie held.

"Oh, so you think you're going to get these, do you?"

Sheba meowed again and rubbed against Jamie's bare ankle.

"You might as well give the scraps to her—she'll drive you crazy until you do." Matt came into the kitchen with the rest of the things from the table.

"All right, here you are." Jamie put the meat scraps into Sheba's dish in the corner, and the white cat totally forgot her usual dignity as she hungrily devoured them.

"Would you like to go for a walk before dark?" Matt asked as Jamie put the last dish into the dishwasher. He'd wiped off the countertops and washed the few pans.

"All right." Jamie walked with him to the patio door again, Sheba following behind. "She wants out too. Is that all right?"

"Sure, she always goes on walks with me. I guess she thinks she's part dog. Do you want to go down by the pond?"

"That sounds nice."

They walked side by side down the sloping

land to the spring-fed pond. The air was warm, but the wind was still gusting intermittently. Jamie was conscious of a complex blend of emotions as she walked so close to Matt. As always his nearness stirred up her emotions.

She felt happy, and at the same time a little unsure of herself—and of him. *Forget all that,* she advised herself, *just enjoy the evening, and don't try to analyze everything all the time.*

## *Chapter Nine*

"*O*h, how beautiful it is tonight." Jamie's voice was soft as they stood on the pond bank. The wind had died down temporarily. A full moon silvered the water, lending an air of unreality to the scene. Matt's small flock of ducks and geese swam over to investigate the disturbance into their territory, the geese honking loudly for a few moments, then subsiding as they realized no threat was present.

"Yes, it is. I love nights like this." Matt's voice, too, was soft as he stood close beside Jamie.

Sheba slunk toward the geese, who hissed at her. She jumped back, hissing herself, then moved on around into the shadows. Jamie laughed, feeling in tune with the whole world at that moment. She sat down on the grassy bank, tucking her feet under her.

In a moment, Matt joined her. "At a time like this, all the trouble in the world seems very far away, doesn't it?" he observed.

Jamie nodded, happy that his mind seemed

so attuned to hers tonight. They sat in a companionable silence for a while, watching the ducks and geese swim back to the middle of the pond, where they spent the night, safe from predators. An occasional rustle in the bushes told of Sheba's prowling investigations.

Matt moved a little closer, and then his arm slid across her shoulders. Jamie leaned her head on his shoulder, her happy, dreamy mood not allowing any of her usual doubts to plague her. It felt so good, so right, to be sitting like this with Matt. As if it were meant to be.

"Your hair smells like fresh air and sunshine," Matt murmured into her ear. "All the things I love." He stroked her hair, running his fingers through its bright strands.

Jamie turned to him, smiling, the dreamy mood still holding her, knowing that he was going to kiss her, and eagerly wanting him to.

Matt pulled her closer to his broad chest, cradling her protectively for a moment before he gently tilted her chin up to look deeply into her eyes. Then he lowered his face to hers and kissed her. The kiss lasted a long time before he finally, reluctantly, pulled away.

Jamie blinked, still caught up in the enchantment of the moment, not wanting it to end. Then, so suddenly she let out a small yelp of surprise, a blur of white landed in her lap.

*Love's Gentle Season* 95

"Sheba!" Matt scolded, laughter in his voice, as the cat settled down and began purring loudly.

Jamie laughed too, a little shakily, and reached down to rub the cat's back. The mood had been broken now, she realized regretfully. They were back in the ordinary everyday world again.

"I don't think you need a dog with Sheba around," Jamie remarked as Sheba arched her back and with one fluid motion moved across to Matt's lap.

"I know what you mean. I miss Bandit, though. I've had him since he was a few weeks old. I wish I could bring him here, but it wouldn't be fair to him."

"What kind of dog is he?" Jamie asked.

"Labrador. Huge, but so friendly he'll lick you to death, like most Labs."

"I've always wanted a dog or cat."

"Well, why don't you get one—or both?"

Jamie considered the suggestion. "Maybe I will. Gram has Prince, of course, but he's her dog completely. It would be nice to have an animal that doted on me the way he does Gram. Of course, I have Dusty and Misty, but that's not quite the same."

Matt laughed. "No, somehow I can't see either of them curling up in your lap and purring." As if to prove his point, Sheba returned to Jamie's lap and began her loud, rusty purr.

This time they both laughed, their eyes meeting and lingering. But things weren't the same as a few moments before, Jamie realized. That elusive enchanted mood wasn't going to come back. Not tonight, anyway.

"Did I tell you I finally managed to buy the land to the west I've been trying to get?"

Matt's unexpected words took Jamie completely by surprise. "No," she said, shaking her head. "You didn't. In fact, since you haven't mentioned it for a while, I thought you'd given up on it."

What did this mean? The small doubt that had never completely left her mind since the night Matt had first kissed her surfaced again: the nagging thought that Matt might be interested in her land, instead of her.

Matt shook his head, his hair gleaming in the moonlight. "No, the owner just couldn't decide if he wanted to sell or not. But last week I finally signed the contract. It will give me an additional two hundred acres."

"That much?" Jamie's voice held surprise. Why, that was twice as much land as she had! Her inner tension began to ease. This meant, it *had* to mean, that she'd been wrong about Matt. He'd never had any designs on her land.

The apparent interest he'd shown in her had to be real—he had to like her for herself.

Matt nodded. "Yes, if I'm going to do any horse breeding here, I need a good bit more grazing area. And this land has been well taken care of. It has a good stand of grass."

"I'm really glad for you, Matt." Jamie gave him a wide smile, feeling light as air suddenly, as if a weight she hadn't even known she was carrying was removed. "That's great!"

He grinned back and got to his feet, holding out a hand to help her up. "I think so too. I thought for a while there the owners weren't going to sell, no matter what I offered."

Sheba leaped off her lap, and Jamie let Matt pull her upright, brushing the loose grass blades from her skirt. He was putting an end to the evening, as he always seemed to do. And he was still leaving her with unanswered questions and doubts.

For even if he'd never had any intentions of trying to acquire her land, that didn't explain why he seemed to be very attracted to her, but yet never said a word to commit himself in any way.

A few minutes ago he'd told her he loved the way her hair smelled like sunshine and fresh air. But he hadn't said anything at all about loving *her*. As they began walking back toward

Matt's house, Jamie firmed her lips. The wind had started again, the gusts blowing her hair into her face, reflecting her mood.

Well, that was all right with her, because she wasn't ready for that kind of a commitment herself, was she? She still hadn't forgotten what had happened with Ted. And besides that, an inner doubt still nagged at her, and she didn't know what it was. One thing she did know, though. She would have to unearth it and come to terms with it before she was ready to hear any words of love from Matt.

As Jamie walked down the lane to the mailbox two days later, the wind buffeted her, almost pushing her along. The hurricane had strengthened considerably since that evening with Matt and was moving northeast. Elinor kept the radio turned on all the time now, and a worried frown creased her brow.

Jamie, unused to hurricanes, was more than worried—she was scared, for the horses, mostly. If it appeared that the storm was going to make landfall somewhere in their area, she and her grandmother could board up the windows, pile some things in the truck, and drive inland far enough to be safe.

But they couldn't take the horses with them. In spite of Matt's and Elinor's assurances that

*Love's Gentle Season* 99

they'd probably be all right, she hated the thought of leaving them to their fate. Even with the notorious unpredictability of hurricanes, the Gulf currents usually kept the storms out of this area, but she was still very uneasy.

She hadn't seen Matt since the evening they'd spent together at his place. She didn't know if he was here or had gone back to Ocala. She kept telling herself she didn't miss him, but she knew that wasn't true. She kept seeing his dark hair, his blue eyes as he'd looked at her that night by the pond.

She reached the mailbox just as Neal Gardner pulled up. He handed her a stack of mail, his pleasant face looking worried too. "Getting ready for Hurricane Edna?" he asked. "Or are you thinking about leaving?"

Jamie shook her head. "We have no plans to leave yet. I hate to leave the horses."

Neal nodded. "I know what you mean. It's hard to know what to do since we don't live in low-lying areas where we'd have no choice. I guess the riding session has been canceled for today—what about their horses?"

"They're going to stay here, along with ours. If it gets really bad, we'll turn them all out to the lower pastures, where it will be safer, everyone keeps saying."

Neal smiled reassuringly. "We'll probably be all right out here, but with a hurricane you don't want to take chances."

"No," Jamie agreed. She waved to Neal and started walking back to the house, leafing through the stack of mail. Ads and bills, the usual, she saw. Then she paused as she came to the last envelope in the stack. That handwriting looked familiar, but she couldn't place it, and there was no return address.

Curious, she tore open the envelope, and pulled out the sheets of paper.

*Dear Jamie,* the letter began.
*I know you'll be surprised to hear from me after all this time. I hope you're not still so angry at me that you won't read this.*

Her eyes widened in shock. The letter was from Ted! They'd broken up three years ago, and she'd never heard from him since. Why was he writing to her now?

Jamie's hand clenched on the letter, crumpling it into a wad. She didn't want to read anything Ted had written. Her mouth tightened and she began walking faster. Ted had made it quite clear three years ago that he was finished with her because of her career choice. He'd hurt her very much.

*Love's Gentle Season*

Then, as she neared the house, her steps slowed, and a tiny thread of curiosity began growing inside her. Why had Ted written after all this time? She walked up on the back porch and sat down in the swing, looking at the wadded paper in her hand for several moments. Should she throw it away without reading it?

No, she finally decided. She was over Ted, had been for a long time. Anything he had to say couldn't hurt her now. She smoothed out the two sheets of paper and began reading where she had left off.

*I want to tell you how sorry I am for what happened between us three years ago. The only excuse I can offer is that I had thought our lives were all planned, for years to come. You threw me for a loop when you told me you were going to quit college and work on the horse farm. I just didn't see how there could be any future for us.*

*I've never forgotten you, Jamie, and I still care for you. I'd like to see you again. If you don't want to see me and don't answer this letter, I'll understand. It's no more than I deserve.*

*But maybe there could still be a future for us after all.*

*Ted*

Jamie finished reading, then stared sightlessly at the rumpled sheets in her hand. The letter was so completely unexpected, she didn't know how to react. For months after she'd given Ted back his ring, she'd hurt every time she thought of him. They'd seemed so close; how could it all have been an illusion on her part, she'd asked herself countless times.

Ted's letter was so reasonable, so plausible. So believable. Her mind went back to the months they'd dated, then become engaged. They'd had fun together. Ted had been very attentive. He'd sent her flowers; he'd never broken a date. Of course, he'd always been very ambitious, but she'd understood that and accepted it. Her entire family was like that, and Ted was single-minded. He'd always known what he wanted. Just as she had.

So why hadn't he been able to accept how much she wanted to breed horses? She'd asked herself that at the time, asked him, and he'd told her she wasn't being realistic, that she had to be sensible.

She glanced down at the letter again. *I still care for you,* Ted had written. *Maybe there could be a future for us after all.* Was he saying that now he could accept her chosen way of life?

And what did it mean to her—anything?

"Any mail?" Elinor opened the screen door and came out on the porch. "Looks as if we may have to start worrying about Edna after all. She's turning toward the east. That means she's heading our way."

Jamie glanced up, her face blank for a moment as she tried to figure out what her grandmother was talking about. Elinor's face held a worried frown. Then Jamie's mind cleared. The hurricane. Heading their way?

Anxiety warred with the uncertainty Ted's letter had aroused. She didn't know how she felt about the letter, but she knew she didn't want to discuss it with her grandmother right now. Besides, they had more important things to worry about.

She hastily rose, scooped up the stack of bills and ads she'd placed on the swing seat, and handed them to Elinor. "Nothing interesting. Do you really think it may come in here, Gram?" As unobtrusively as possible, she folded Ted's letter and tried to replace it in its envelope.

It was too rumpled, she realized, feeling her face redden. To heck with it. She pushed the sheets and envelope into the pocket of her jeans, and glanced up to see her grandmother's eyes on her.

"We haven't had one come in here for a long time, but it's always possible." Her grandmother gave her a curious look, but didn't say anything more.

Relieved, Jamie knew she wouldn't pry. She'd wait until Jamie was ready to talk about it. "Well, then, I guess we'd better get ready for it. Do you think we need to board up the windows, or just tape them?"

Elinor gave her a wry smile. "I don't like the sound of this lady. Let's board them up."

Jamie nodded. "All right. I think there are enough boards left in the barn to do it. What else?"

"We already have enough canned food and some jugs of water, but we'd better fill the bathtub, in case some lines get broken. You'd better go to the store and get a gallon of kerosene and some candles, in case the power goes off. Oh, yes, and flashlight batteries."

Jamie looked at her. "I was going to ask if you thought we should stay or leave. I guess you just answered that question."

"We're up on high ground, no danger of flooding here. It would take a real granddaddy of a hurricane to reach us through that stand of trees. And I don't want to leave the horses."

Jamie nodded. "Neither do I. All right, let's get to work."

"You'd better get the kerosene and candles first. Those things go fast when there's a hurricane scare. You may have to go into Pensacola."

Jamie discovered her grandmother was right. The small country store was filled with people, all in a hurry, and all with an anxious look in their eyes. She got the last of the flashlight batteries, and the candles were already gone. A group of people clustered around the meat counter, buying cold cuts. She'd better get some too, she decided.

A sense of urgency pervaded the atmosphere, and Jamie felt her own stomach tightening as she tried to wait patiently. Ted's letter was still in her pocket, and every time she moved it crackled, reminding her of things she'd rather forget—thought she *had* forgotten. She didn't have time to worry about Ted now.

She wished Matt were here, she realized. Somehow she'd feel better knowing he was just across the fields and not several hundred miles away. Maybe he was. No, she dismissed that thought. He'd have been in touch with them before now, she felt sure. Of course, maybe he was as busy as they were, getting ready for the storm. She didn't have time to worry about Matt, either, she told herself.

As an afterthought, she picked up a couple of bags of ice. If the electricity went out, they'd need them for the cooler.

Hurrying to the truck, she glanced at the sky. It was completely overcast now, the gusts of wind getting stronger. Kerosene! She'd almost forgotten it. She also filled the truck with gas, trying not to think why she was doing it. Maybe they'd have to leave after all. She debated going on in to Pensacola to try to find candles, then decided against it. Time was more important. They probably had some around somewhere. If not, they had the kerosene lamps. And, she hoped, they wouldn't need any of it.

Elinor already had brought a stack of boards from the barn, and was busily working on the kitchen windows, which faced north, the direction the storm would come in from if it came.

"Why didn't you wait for me?" Jamie asked, hurrying up on the porch.

"Thought I'd better get started."

Jamie took the supplies inside, then came back out. "Here, give me that hammer. You hold the other end of the board."

"I'm not helpless, Jamie," Elinor said crisply.

"I'm well aware of that, but I'm younger and maybe a little more limber." Jamie grinned at her grandmother, holding out her hand for the hammer.

Elinor gave it to her, her lips pursed. "I'm not so sure about that."

"Neither am I, but I can't stand here and watch you do the heavy work."

"Before we're through here, I imagine we'll both have enough to do."

"I'm afraid you're right," Jamie agreed.

They both worked hard all afternoon. After they finished boarding the windows, they brought in the porch furniture and took the swing off its hooks, so the wind wouldn't bang it against the house. While her grandmother filled the lamps with kerosene, Jamie walked around outside giving everything a last check.

The weather news had grown steadily more ominous. Edna was moving north-northeast. All low-lying areas had already been evacuated, and the periodic bulletins about the crowded emergency shelters in the schools made Jamie thankful their land was so high. But were they foolish to stay on?

As she fastened the toolshed door more securely, she glanced at the horses, knowing her and Elinor's decision to stay was based mainly on the fact that they couldn't take the animals. She fed them, then opened the lower gates, turning them into the fields near the protective stand of trees. As she watched Misty, her brows drew together in a worried frown. It was only a few weeks until Misty was due to foal. She hoped this emergency didn't start everything early.

The sky had gradually darkened to an ominous charcoal, the storm clouds roiling as the day ended and evening came. The knot of tension in Jamie's stomach had hardened until it hurt. She stood watching the horses as they moved down to the lower fields. They seemed to feel the threat too, and instinctively knew the safest place to go.

She wished Matt were here. Why did he have to be gone now? She shrugged impatiently. She couldn't depend on Matt. She and her grandmother had to depend on themselves—or leave. Maybe they should. Was she risking Elinor's life and her own by staying?

*Wait a minute,* she reminded herself. *You didn't make this decision alone, you know. You probably couldn't drag Gram out of here with a rope.*

She went back to the house to find Elinor lis-

## Love's Gentle Season 109

tening to a weather bulletin, her forehead creased in a frown. She turned as Jamie entered the kitchen. "It's still headed our way, and it will probably make landfall sometime tonight. Jamie, maybe we should have left."

Jamie felt the knot of tension clench her stomach muscles. As long as her grandmother hadn't been overly worried, she'd been able to keep her own anxiety in check. "We can still leave," she said, making her voice firm.

Elinor shook her head. "No, it would be more dangerous to leave now. The roads out of here are too crowded. We could get stranded—maybe not find a place to stay because all the motels will be full too."

Jamie swallowed and straightened her shoulders. "Well, then, I guess we'll just have to settle in and wait it out."

Elinor grinned, her frown smoothing out. "We've had lots of storms before, and this old house is strong and solid. I wonder if Matt's here or in Ocala. If he's here, we should call and tell him to come over here and wait with us. That house of his has so much glass."

Jamie hadn't thought of that. Worry for Matt's safety filled her. "I'll try to call him," she said, heading for the wall phone. Matt's phone rang and rang with no answer. Jamie finally hung up. "He could be outside." She made a quick decision. "I'm going to drive over there and see."

Elinor nodded. "Yes, you'd better. But, Jamie, be careful, and hurry back. The wind is really picking up now."

"I will, Gram." Jamie gave her a brief hug, then hurried out to the pickup. Uneasily wishing she'd left before dark, she switched on the truck's lights. Since the road dead-ended at Matt's place, there was no traffic, and Jamie had no idea what her neighbors were doing—whether most of them had decided to leave after all, or stay. *Not that it matters,* she told herself. But still, she'd feel better knowing that they weren't the only ones left to weather the storm.

She'd feel better if *Matt* were here, she admitted, pulling up before his house. Matt's dusk-to-dawn light on its high pole illuminated the area. Everything had a deserted look. Matt's Jeep wasn't in its usual place beside the closed garage door, and there was no board or tape on any of the windows in the house. *He must be in Ocala,* she thought, feeling a sense of letdown at the realization. Then she saw a flash of white at a front window.

Sheba! Jamie couldn't leave the cat alone here in the coming storm. Sheba would be terrified. But how could she get into the house?

Maybe Matt had left a key somewhere for his housekeeper. No, she decided, that wasn't likely. The housekeeper no doubt had her own key.

But maybe he'd left a spare key anyway. It was worth a search, because Sheba had seen her and was now walking back and forth across the windowsill. Jamie couldn't hear her cries, but she could tell that the cat was meowing frantically. She got out of the truck, struggling to close the door against a sudden violent gust of wind, and walked over to the house. She felt over the top of the door, but found no key.

Looking around for another likely hiding place, she spotted two large flowerpots, one on each side of the door. But a quick search failed to turn up a key in either of them. She couldn't go off and leave the cat alone. "Hang in there, Sheba, I'm coming," she told the now almost frantic cat, smiling reassuringly, hoping the animal understood.

Maybe she'd be lucky enough to find a back window unlocked, she told herself, hurrying around to the back of the house, but her hopes were dim. Matt wasn't likely to be that careless. She was right. She made the rounds, trying each window, but all were securely locked.

Biting her lip, she jammed her wind-whipped hair more securely under her sweatshirt hood and considered her options. There were only two: She could leave the cat there and go home, hoping Matt would soon arrive—or she could break into the house and rescue her.

"Oh, no!" she groaned aloud, but she knew which choice it would be. A sliding glass door opened onto the patio in back. She wasn't going to smash that. It would have to be a window. She looked around for something to use, considering a tree branch the wind had blown down at her feet. No, not strong enough, she decided. Too bad Matt didn't have a rock garden, because rocks were in short supply in Florida. Maybe there would be something in the garage she could pry with or use to smash a pane of glass. Except that the garage would also undoubtedly be locked.

She tried the garage door, and to her amazement found it unlocked. Jamie slid it open, and looked around for something to use. A large toolbox stood in the corner. She skirted Matt's gleaming black Porsche, and opened the box. A pipe wrench? She could smash a window with that for sure.

She picked up the wrench and closed the toolbox. She walked back outside and pulled the garage door down. As she turned toward the house, she heard the sound of a vehicle ap-

*Love's Gentle Season* 113

proaching. Matt! It had to be Matt. She felt a smile curve her mouth, and the knot of tension in her stomach loosened a little.

Matt's Jeep turned the last bend in the road and came to a stop in the drive. The door opened and Matt got out. He threw a quick glance at her pickup, then started walking fast to the front door.

"Matt!" Jamie called. "I'm here." She hurried toward him, her smile widening, an irrational feeling filling her that now everything would be all right, even as a gust of wind nearly knocked her over.

Oh, she was glad Matt was here!

"Jamie, what are you doing here?" A relieved smile broke out on Matt's tanned face, erasing his worried frown. He walked toward her, and they met halfway. "You should be home." His eyes swept over her briefly, then gazed into her own again for a long, intent moment.

Jamie felt warmed by his smile and glance, and her feeling that now things were going to be all right intensified. She pushed her wind-tossed hair under her hood again. "I came over to see if you were here. I wanted to ask you to come and stay at our house—it's safer. Then I saw Sheba, and—" She gestured with the wrench. "It's a good thing you got home when you did. In another five minutes, you'd be minus a pane of glass in a back window."

Another hard gust of wind buffeted them. Matt reached out to steady Jamie, and his hand stayed on her shoulder, his jeans and jacket molded to his powerful frame. His smile faded, the frown returning. "Thanks, Jamie, but I can't do that. I was delayed in Ocala, and I've got to see to the horses and get some windows taped. This hurricane looks bad. Here, I'll take that." He removed his hand from Jamie's shoulder, holding it out for the wrench.

Jamie gave it to him, and he put it in a deep front pocket of his jacket. He took a key ring out of his pocket as he walked toward the front door.

"Yes, you can," Jamie said firmly, keeping up with him. "Here, give me the key, and I'll start on the windows while you see to the horses." They'd reached the front steps by now, and she held out her hand. Her shoulder, even under the sweatshirt, still tingled from his touch.

"You don't have to—" Matt paused, his voice tight with anxiety, and looked at her. He smiled briefly, then handed her the key ring. "All right—the masking tape is under the sink. I'll be back to help you as soon as I let the horses into the lower field."

"I was just going to remind you that neighbors help each other, as you've so often told me. Go on, I'll find it." A vicious gust of wind almost knocked her off her feet again. She grabbed for the doorknob, then unlocked the door as Matt moved quickly behind her to shield her.

"Get inside," Matt yelled, shouting to be heard above the wind. "You'd better start with these big windows in front. I'll be back in a minute." He disappeared around the corner of the house.

Jamie slammed the door on another strong blast, and headed for the kitchen, with Sheba rubbing frantically against her and purring loudly. "Yes, I know, it's scary." Jamie bent down to give the cat a reassuring stroke down her back. "But we'll be all right."

She'd better feed Sheba to keep her out from underfoot, she decided, locating a can of cat food in the refrigerator. "There you go." She spooned some into Sheba's dish, and left the cat eating while she got the tape. She'd also need a stool or chair. A folded step stool stood in the corner.

Jamie hurried back to the living room and started on the big front windows. Now that Matt was no longer with her, her tenseness was back full force. Her fingers stuck to the tape, and she fumbled and dropped the roll.

Several hard wind gusts rattled the heavy tempered glass before she finally finished. The tape would keep the windows from shattering, but not from breaking. But would it hold if the storm got really bad? She didn't know, but she was determined to talk Matt into coming home with her.

"There." She finished placing the last diagonal strip, then drew the heavy draperies closed. The storm was coming from this direction, so she'd better do the windows on this side first. She went out into the entry, and crossed it. The next room was Matt's bedroom, she guessed, noticing its brown bedspread and masculine-looking furnishings.

She was halfway through the first window when she heard the front door open, then close. "I'm in here, Matt," she called, not stopping her taping. The sense of urgency she felt was increasing by the minute.

She turned to give Matt a quick smile as she heard him enter the room. His brows were still drawn together, his jaw muscles tight. He carried another roll of tape.

"I'll do this one," he said briefly, pulling off a strip of tape as he reached the window. "I want to get these front ones first."

## Love's Gentle Season         117

Again Matt's presence relieved some of her anxiety. Her fingers steadied, and she felt a sense of companionship with Matt working in the same room with her. As soon as they finished, they hurried to the other bedroom in the front, and in a few minutes had taped those too. Having gobbled her snack, Sheba now followed them.

"I think the back will be all right, but I'd better tape the patio door," Matt told Jamie. "Maybe we should do the eastern windows too."

"I'll start on those while you do the door." Jamie hurried off to the bathroom, Sheba following closely behind, rubbing against her ankles. Jamie stopped to stroke her. "It's all right," she reassured the nervous cat, grinning wryly at her choice of words.

Another half hour and they were finished. Matt replaced the tape under the sink and straightened up. He let out a relieved breath. "At least that's done. Now all we can do is wait Edna out and hope she misses us."

Jamie was reminded suddenly of the other conversation they'd had about the hurricane two days ago, and of that wonderful, dreamy time by the pond later. She brushed the thoughts aside. This was no time for that.

"And you're going to wait it out with us," she said firmly.

Matt gave her a tired grin. "All right, I won't argue with you now. I would feel safer in that old house of yours than here. Do you have plenty of kerosene and candles?" As if to underscore his words, the electricity flickered once, twice, then steadied, as another hard gust of wind buffeted the house.

Jamie swallowed nervously. "Kerosene, yes; candles, no. The store was sold out."

"I'll get some." Matt opened a drawer and took out several packages of emergency candles. "I have a feeling we're going to need these."

"Me too." Her sense of urgency was intense now. She shouldn't have left her grandmother alone. She wanted to get back to the solid old farmhouse.

Matt put some cans of cat food in a bag, then scooped up Sheba. "All right, let's go."

Jamie followed him outside and got into her truck. Matt turned his Jeep around, and she followed him down the curving lane, wincing as she watched the treetops swaying in the wind, bending so far down, it looked as if they'd snap in half.

*Chapter Ten*

*J*ust as Jamie and Matt pulled into her driveway, the porch light flickered, then went out—and stayed out. Jamie slid out of the truck and hurried to Matt's Jeep. He was already out too, having a hard time holding on to a squirming Sheba as well as the bag of cat food and candles.

"Here, give me that." Jamie reached for the bag, and they made their way across the yard toward the house. As they reached the back-porch steps, she saw a small, wavery light through a crack in the boarded kitchen window, and the darkness didn't feel quite so intense now.

Elinor opened the door before they got to it. "About time you got here," she scolded. "I was about to come and see what had happened to you." She stepped back so they could enter, and the first drops of rain splattered on the porch steps.

Compunction hit Jamie, mingling with her anxiety. "I'm sorry, Gram, I forgot to call to let you know what was going on. Matt got home while I was there, and we had to tape the windows." Her grandmother had lit two lamps, Jamie saw, but their feeble glow didn't do much to dissipate the darkness.

Matt put Sheba down, and Prince at once walked over to investigate. The cat arched her back and hissed, backing off from the dog's curious nose. Prince retreated too, as if knowing when to leave well enough alone.

The rain was coming down hard now, the wind gusts splattering it against the windows. Jamie felt the knot in her stomach getting bigger. How bad would it get? "What's the latest on the hurricane?"

Elinor looked worried. "They did an update right before you got here. It's still headed north-northeast. It could hit here or anywhere in a hundred-mile area. All the shelters are full, and they're telling people who haven't already left to stay put now."

"I wouldn't want to be out in that. But the horses—" Jamie turned to Matt. "Do you think they'll be all right?"

He shrugged, his face set in worried lines. "I hope so. We've done all we can. They're safer in the fields. They'll stay down by the tree windbreak."

"I guess we should go into the living room,"

## Love's Gentle Season 121

Elinor said, "as it's the side away from the storm." She picked up one of the lamps and moved toward the other room.

Matt took the other one and followed her. Jamie scooped up the battery-operated radio from the table and came behind. Sheba, meowing plaintively, trailed her. Prince was already settled under his favorite rocker. Jamie saw her grandmother had pulled the living-room draperies tightly closed and pinned them together.

Elinor placed her lamp on top of the old upright piano. She turned to Matt. "You'd better put that one here too," she directed, "away from the animals."

Matt complied, turning to give Jamie a reassuring smile, as if he knew how tense she felt.

Jamie smiled back, feeling the knot in her stomach ease a little. She set the radio on the maple coffee table and, after picking up Sheba, sat down on the sofa.

"You two must be starving," Elinor said. "I kept some supper hot for you. I'll bring it in here."

Jamie put Sheba on the floor and got up. "That sounds great, but I'll get it. You sit down and rest." She got one of the lamps from the piano.

"I'll help." Matt followed her back to the kitchen.

The wind and rain were driving down with more force now. Jamie shivered as she placed the lamp on the table, relieved they'd boarded the windows in here. Two plates of pork chops and mashed potatoes and gravy were in the oven of the propane-gas stove, keeping warm. Now, how had her grandmother known Matt would come back with her? Jamie shrugged, lifting them out with a pot holder, and handed one to Matt.

Another hard blast of wind rattled the windows, and the kitchen suddenly seemed almost cozy in the small, yellow glow of the kerosene lamp. She and Matt here, closed in from the storm. . . . She shook her head. This was no time for such notions. "I guess we'd better go back to the living room," she said.

"Oh, I think we're safe in here for a few minutes." Matt's voice was easy and calm now. He put his plate down on the big oak table and smiled at her.

Inexplicably she felt better, her tension easing a little. "All right." She smiled back, putting her plate down across from his. "Do you want some coffee?"

Matt nodded. "I could use about three cups of Elinor's brew right now. It's a long drive from Ocala, and I was worried the whole trip

## Love's Gentle Season       123

about getting home in time to let the horses out." He pulled out a chair and sat down.

Jamie poured coffee into two cups and got out milk from the refrigerator. *Home.* He'd called his place here home. Did he feel that way, or was it just an expression? "I would have let them out if you hadn't come when you did." She sat down too.

"I wasn't sure you knew I was gone." He picked up his knife and fork and cut the meat.

"Well, I thought you were, since you hadn't called in the last two days." Jamie bit her lip. Why had she said that? Now Matt would think she kept tabs on him, expected him to call every day. She hurriedly picked up her own fork, not looking at him.

But instead of picking up on it and giving her a teasing query about missing him, as she expected, Matt was silent for a minute. "Thanks for coming over and taking care of things," he said finally. "I really appreciate it."

"That's what neighbors are for, remember?" Jamie said lightly, feeling a little let down at his reply. "And anyway I hadn't done anything yet when you got back."

"You would have, though—you looked as if you were ready to get serious with that wrench." He glanced over at her, his dark eyes amused.

Jamie shrugged, managing a smile. "I've never broken into a house before, and I wasn't looking forward to it. I was sure glad you showed up." Did he know just how glad she'd been? *Cool it,* she advised herself. Hadn't she decided only two days ago, down by the pond, that it wasn't time yet for anything serious between them? And wasn't she relieved that Matt wasn't pushing anything?

She moved, and heard a crackle of paper in her pocket. For a second she wondered what it was, then she remembered. *Ted's letter.* She shifted again, uneasily, and the paper crackled once more. All the turmoil she'd felt this morning when she had read it returned. Why hadn't she just thrown it away? Torn it into a hundred pieces and tossed it into the trash? *I didn't have time,* she told herself. But she'd had time. She hadn't wanted to, that was the truth.

She'd wanted to think about what Ted had written. Consider it. Then she was furious at herself. She couldn't really be considering giving Ted a second chance after the way he'd treated her. She had more sense than that, surely! But, deep inside, a little voice reminded her that all that had happened three years ago. People could change a lot in three years. And Ted had sounded as if he were truly sorry.

Jamie concentrated on eating, not looking at

Matt. The letter felt as if it were burning a hole in her pocket. She wanted to finish eating, take the letter to her bedroom, and hide it away in a dresser drawer. A hard gust of wind slammed against the house, finding its way through the cracks in the boards, and rattling the windows fiercely.

She threw a quick, uneasy glance toward them. Would the boards hold if the storm increased its fury? And what if the hurricane actually hit them? She closed her eyes to blot out that thought. No boards in the world could protect this house if that happened. She opened her eyes to find Matt looking at her, and for a moment their glances held. Jamie looked down first.

Matt pushed back his chair and picked up his plate and cup. "Let's go back into the living room," he suggested, walking across to the sink to deposit his dishes in it.

*No matter how much he pretends otherwise, Matt is worried.* That thought made a stab of fear plunge through her. If Matt was worried, then there was something to worry about. She rose and took her dishes to the sink. Matt was pouring himself another cup of coffee.

"Do you want more too?" he turned to ask her.

The frown was gone, but Jamie had the uneasy feeling he was making a deliberate effort to keep her from seeing how he really felt. She nodded. "Yes. I'll go see if Gram wants a cup."

She walked to the living-room doorway. Elinor was sitting in her rocker, her head against the seat back, her eyes closed, lines of exhaustion on her face. Prince slept under the chair, and Sheba was curled up on her lap. One of Elinor's hands, the veins showing in the thin skin, rested on the cat's back.

Jamie drew a deep breath, anxiety hitting her anew. Her grandmother wasn't a young woman anymore, no matter how active and healthy she still was. She should be out of this.

Jamie turned back to the kitchen, her own brows knit, biting her lip in vexation at herself. She glanced up at Matt, still standing by the coffeepot. She shook her head. "No, she's asleep, and I hope she stays that way. I could just kick myself that I didn't insist we leave while we still could."

She walked over to the stove and accepted the cup of coffee Matt held out to her, her lips pressed together.

"Don't be so hard on yourself," Matt said as he picked up the lamp and they moved toward the living room. "You know as well as I do that Elinor isn't going anywhere she doesn't want to. And she didn't want to leave."

"Yes, I know, but I should have insisted. I should have—" She stopped and gave Matt a wry smile. "You're right, short of hog-tying her and carrying her out, there's not much I could have done. But the point is, I didn't realize how bad it was going to get."

She reached the couch, put her cup on the coffee table and sat down. Matt returned the lamp to the piano, then sat down beside her.

"Neither did I," Matt answered. "And we still may not get much damage." He reached over and switched on the radio, keeping the volume low so as not to wake Elinor.

In spite of her growing anxiety, Jamie was very conscious of Matt's presence. The warmth from his strong body seemed to reach out to her, and some of her worry and anxiety eased again. She leaned close to the radio, and her arm brushed against Matt's shoulder, increasing the feeling.

" . . . Power is out everywhere now. We've switched to emergency generators." Even through the weak, static-filled broadcast, the tenseness of the disembodied voice came through clearly. "Edna is projected to be only an hour or two from making landfall, some. . . ." A burst of static drowned out the announcer's next words, then his voice could be heard again. " . . . we'll stay on the air as long as possible, to give you further—" Another burst of static interrupted, and then the radio went dead. Matt reached over and switched it off.

Jamie's fear was back, tenfold. She swallowed, glancing over to see if her grandmother had awakened. No, she still slept as if totally exhausted. Jamie reached for her coffee cup and saw that her hands were shaking. Quickly she put it down again.

She turned to Matt, not caring now if her fear showed in her face. "What's going to happen now, Matt?"

Why, oh, why, Jamie asked herself, hadn't they gotten out of here? It wouldn't save the horses if they died too. Even though she didn't know anything directly about the fury of a hurricane, she'd read enough accounts of their potential for devastating destruction to realize the danger they faced.

"We're quite a distance from the water, and we have that band of forest to further protect us, even if Edna makes landfall in this area." Matt repeated what he and Elinor had said before, his voice calm and reassuring. His warm, strong hand reached over to cover her twisting fists. Slowly, gently, he pulled her fingers apart and massaged them until she began to relax.

She gave him a level look, taking a deep

breath. "Then all we can do is wait, is that it?" Her voice was still tight with anxiety, but she was grateful it sounded firm and steady now. She had her panic under control, and Matt's hand covering hers was infinitely comforting.

Matt nodded. "Essentially, that's it. We're in the safest part of the house, away from the direction of the storm. And the wind isn't getting any stronger, have you noticed? That's a good sign."

Jamie nodded slowly, feeling her stomach muscles relaxing as some of her tension eased. He was right, the gusts of wind and rain buffeting the house didn't seem to have gotten any worse in the last few minutes.

"Well, what's Edna doing now?" Elinor's voice erupted into a sudden lull in the storm.

Jamie jumped, her taut nerves instinctively reacting. She glanced at her grandmother. Elinor was fully awake, her dark eyes snapping alertly. She sat straight up in the rocker now, her hand automatically soothing Sheba.

Jamie shrugged, not wanting to tell the older woman what the radio announcer had said a few minutes before. "They're still not sure where it's going to come in," she said evasively.

"But it doesn't sound too good for us," Elinor said, shrewdly filling in the missing pieces. "Well, this is a sound old house. It's weathered one hurricane that was pretty close, and it's still standing."

Another hard gust of wind and rain rattled the boarded-up windows of the kitchen. Jamie tensed, but again, it didn't seem any worse than before. Maybe it was going to be all right, after all.

"Do you want some coffee, Gram—Matt?" Jamie asked, getting up. Her own cup was empty, she saw, wondering when she'd finished it.

"Yes, I do, but I'll get it," Elinor answered. "I need to stretch my legs." Sheba jumped out of her lap before she could lift her down.

"I could use some too." Matt handed his cup to Jamie, his smile warm and reassuring.

Jamie returned his smile, wondering how she'd ever have made it through this siege without his presence. She picked up a flashlight from the coffee table, instead of bothering with the lamp this time, and she and Elinor went to the kitchen.

Jamie reached for the coffeepot and shook it. "I guess I'd better make some more," she remarked, smiling at her grandmother.

A sudden tremendous blast of wind-driven rain roared up from the fields below, hitting the boarded-up windows like a giant fist. Jamie dropped the coffeepot onto the countertop with a bang and jumped back. The flashlight had fallen onto the floor and rolled, its beams shooting wildly.

She hadn't heard him come in, but Matt was beside them, scooping up the flashlight. "Come on, get in here, quick!" His voice was tight with urgency as they all three moved quickly into the living room. He swiftly blew out the lamps, then maneuvered them under the framework of the open doorway into the hall. "Crouch down," he urged, sliding between them, one strong arm around each of the women, holding them into a compact huddle.

Another fierce blast of rain and wind hit the house, and this time Jamie could feel it shake. Fear shot through her. The old house wasn't going to stand after all. They were all going to die! Numbness overtook her as they crouched in the pitch-blackness, listening to the storm batter the house for what seemed like hours.

"It's letting up. It's passed over us."

Matt's voice penetrated Jamie's fog of fear, but for a minute she couldn't believe what he was saying. Then she realized the buffets of wind and rain had slackened to what seemed merely a normal storm. It was over? The house was still standing? They weren't going to die after all?

Slowly, shakily, she stood, groping in the

darkness for her grandmother. "Gram? Are you all right?" She made contact with Elinor's hand, and squeezed it.

Elinor squeezed Jamie's hand in return. "Sure am." Her voice cracked a little, but then she steadied it. "Didn't think that young lady, Edna, could do this old house in."

Jamie felt Matt move away from her, then heard his footsteps as he walked across the room. Then she heard the raspy sound of a match being rubbed against the box, and a second later, the weak but welcome flare of the kerosene lamp flickered to life.

She let out her breath, then inhaled deeply, wincing at the sudden pain in her chest. She must have been holding her breath most of the time without realizing it.

"Well, do you suppose it's safe to go make that coffee now?" Elinor grinned at them both and, after lighting the second lamp, took it with her to the kitchen.

Jamie's eyes met Matt's, a relieved grin curving up both their mouths. Then Jamie's eyes widened. "The horses! Oh, Matt, what do you suppose happened to them? We have to go see if they're all right." She whirled, her muscles poised for flight.

Matt's hand on her shoulder stopped her. "Wait a few minutes to see if this isn't just a lull. I think the eye missed us completely and we got the outer winds, but if not—"

He didn't have to finish the sentence. Jamie swallowed, realizing they still weren't safe. "If not, we're in for it." She changed her purposeful stride and went to the stove to help Elinor with the coffee.

They drank it standing in the living room for safety's sake, listening tensely for signs that the storm was going to start up again in all its fury. But it didn't. As the minutes passed, the rain gradually lessened to a steady downpour, interspersed with scaled-down gusts of wind.

Matt put his cup on the coffee table. He glanced at Jamie. "I think now we can go see if the horses are all right."

Jamie nodded, and five minutes later, covered with hooded slickers and carrying flashlights, they stepped off the porch into the rain.

"I don't think anything very big hit the house." Matt swung his flashlight around in a wide arc, then up at the roof. Jamie's eyes followed it as the beam of light caught sparkles from the rain. Pine needles, leaves, and tree limbs littered the roof, but none had been big enough to do any real damage, she saw, relieved.

Elinor stood in the open doorway, her expression anxious. "It's all right, Gram," Jamie told her. "No damage. At least on this side."

They walked around the house and found only a shutter torn off its hinges. Then they headed down toward the lower fields.

Jamie's sneakers were soon soaked through, but she hardly noticed, as she strained for a glimpse of the horses. Since they were all dark colored, she knew she and Matt would have to get very close before they saw them.

Fear for the safety of the animals filled her as they proceeded and she saw the full extent of the destruction the storm had caused. Pine needles, leaves, and entire tree limbs carpeted the ground. The barn door swung in the diminishing wind, hanging by one hinge, and the first gate was blown completely down, Jamie saw, her fear increasing. She turned to Matt, reaching for the reassurance of his touch with her free hand.

His hand, wet from the rain, which had slowed to a fine mist, squeezed hers. "Don't worry. They're probably fine."

His touch was comforting, but Jamie heard the tenseness in his voice. He was worried too. The second gate was still securely closed, she saw with amazement. They opened it and left it propped open for the horses to come back up now.

They were halfway down through the far field when Jamie caught a glimpse of something moving. She turned her flashlight on it, her heart in her throat, half afraid to look. Then she let out her breath in a long sigh of relief. Her flashlight beam, joined by Matt's, showed all six of the horses walking toward them.

"They seem to be fine." Matt's voice sounded relieved too, as he swung his flashlight beam over each horse in turn. "But they want to get back to the barn." That was obvious as the animals changed their walk to a trot when they saw the gate was now open.

Jamie and Matt followed along behind, giving them one last check when they were in their stalls. "Just a few scratches, that's all," Matt said in satisfaction. "I told you they would get into the safest place." He turned to Jamie with a grin, and they started back toward the house.

She smiled too, saying, "Now let's go check on yours."

"You don't have to come along," Matt said. "I can go alone."

Jamie shook her head. "Neighbors help each other, remember?" Somehow, that old phrase, after what they'd experienced together tonight, didn't sound right. She turned to him, even though he was only a dim outline in the dark.

"*Friends* help each other." That didn't express her true feelings either, she thought.

Matt had turned toward her too. She saw his hooded head nod. "All right. I'd like to have you come along, Jamie."

What did that mean, she wondered as they walked the rest of the way in silence. Just its face value? She dismissed her speculations, as this was no time or place for anything but friendship. They stopped by the house to tell Elinor the good news, then headed down the porch steps again.

"Come on, we'll take the Jeep," Matt said. "I don't think we'll need to use the four-wheel drive, but it's possible."

The road was littered with branches, pine needles, and leaves too, and as they rounded a bend on Matt's lane, he brought the Jeep to a sudden, screeching stop.

One of the big slash pines had fallen directly across the road, effectively ending it for the time being. Jamie felt her muscles tense, her hands clenching into fists. She hoped that didn't mean the damage was more extensive here. She and Matt opened their doors at the same time and got out.

"I can move that with a chain hooked onto the Jeep tomorrow," Matt said as they stepped over it. "I hope there's nothing worse than this," he added, echoing her unspoken thoughts as they started walking.

They rounded the last curve, and Jamie drew in her breath as Matt swung his flashlight beam over the front of the house. Even from this distance she could see jagged splinters of glass glinting in the beams of light, a dark gaping hole in the middle. "Oh, Matt!" she gasped. "I hope your house isn't ruined!"

A feeble sliver of moon now fitfully appeared between the clouds. As Jamie looked at him, it showed her Matt's face, his jaw tight as they hurried closer.

"I do too, but right now, I'm more worried about the horses."

They almost jogged around the house and then down into the fields. Just as at her place, the upper gate was down, and almost at once, she saw his stallion, Smoke, because of his light gray color. As they got closer, Jamie saw the two mares standing close to him.

Matt swung his flashlight over them. "They're all right."

Jamie heard his deep, relieved sigh. In another five minutes they had reassured themselves that Matt's animals had weathered the hurricane too.

"Smoke needs this cut disinfected, though,"

Matt said. "I'll turn them into the barn, then go get some stuff."

Now that the crisis was over, Jamie became aware of how cold, wet, and tired she was. Her soaked sneakers had numbed her feet, and enough rain had gotten through the slicker to make her shiver with chill.

She followed Matt back to the house, neither of them openly speculating on what they might find there, but Jamie bit her lip as they entered the back door. Only one of the big front windows had broken, she saw, relieved. The rain and wind damage from the shattered pane had been partly stopped by the heavy drapes, which still hung, but were slashed and torn.

"I'm glad I decided not to put carpeting in here," Matt said lightly, his voice sounding as relieved as she felt. The rain had pooled on the hardwood floor in places, but it hadn't reached the oriental area rug. Jamie helped him roll it up and put it in the far corner of the room.

"I'll mop up this water while you tend to Smoke," she offered. "Unless you need me to help."

"You don't have to clean up this mess, and I could use some help," he said. "Smoke is the most gentle stallion I've ever known, but he may be jumpy tonight, after what he's been

## Love's Gentle Season 139

through." His eyes found hers and the glance held.

"All right," Jamie answered. Now that the crisis was over, she felt the breathless mix of emotions Matt always aroused in her.

Matt found antiseptic and filled a pail with hot water. They walked together back to the barn.

Jamie saw the first faint rosy tints of dawn on the horizon. The long night was almost over, she realized, relief filling her. It was one she wouldn't forget in a hurry.

In a few minutes they were finished. They walked back to the Jeep, and Matt drove her home. It was full daylight now, and Jamie felt her heavy eyelids drooping in the steamy warmth of the vehicle's interior.

Had she ever been this tired in her life? Matt braked the Jeep in her driveway, and she opened her eyes reluctantly, turning to him with a tired smile. "Do you want to come in for some coffee and breakfast?"

He shook his head, his answering smile as tired as hers. "I've got to get back and start cleaning up the mess. Do you need any help here?"

"No," Jamie said, struggling to keep her eyes open. "I'm going to feed the horses, then get a few hours' sleep before I try to do anything else. We can have a joint cleanup of both places, if you want."

"All right," Matt said, giving her a tired smile. "That sounds good to me too." He moved closer to Jamie, and before she realized what he had in mind, he bent and gave her a quick, hard kiss. "Sleep well—and I'll see you soon."

Jamie watched him leave, his kiss tingling on her lips, and the slightly raspy feel of his cheek against hers lingering. After the cleanup was finished, would she see him "soon," or would he go off to Ocala on one of his ever-more-frequent trips?

Their relationship seemed to have reached some kind of plateau. She knew she cared for Matt, but there was still some kind of a barrier between them that she didn't understand—on both their parts.

She went inside. The house was quiet, and Prince came to greet her. She saw Elinor asleep on the couch, an afghan pulled over her, her face exhausted looking.

She'd left a note propped up on the coffee table: *I've fed the horses—the cleanup can wait. Go and take a nap.*

She'd do just that, Jamie decided, going slowly and tiredly to her room, yawning as she went. She was too tired even to shower. As she removed her jeans, a crackle of paper caused her to wonder for a minute—then she remembered.

Ted's letter. She pulled it out and looked at the crumpled pages, then tossed them into the wastebasket. After a moment, she took them out again, and stuck them into a dresser drawer, not quite sure why.

She only knew some instinctive feeling told her she and Ted weren't finished with each other yet, as she'd thought before. Maybe that was what was wrong between her and Matt. Could it be Ted was right—there might be a future for them after all? No! She instantly rejected that thought.

Ted's kisses had never made her feel the way Matt's did. Still, once she had loved Ted. Could she be absolutely sure that that love was completely dead?

Tonight's events had made her feel closer to Matt than ever before, but something was holding her back from any kind of a real commitment, even in her own mind. Just as she sensed that same holding back in him. She didn't understand it, but she knew that it had to be settled, once and for all, before the impasse between them could ever be resolved.

## Chapter Eleven

Jamie went into the kitchen and plopped down onto a chair with an exhausted sigh. "I think I've combed every grass blade on the farm, Gram."

Elinor shook her head. "I don't know why you've been knocking yourself out for the last week, Jamie. After all, it's only your parents and sister coming. Not the President."

Jamie shot her a tired grin. "I think I'd rather have the President. You know what perfectionists Mom and Dad are—and Linda too."

"So? It's your place, Jamie, not theirs. Don't forget that. You've done a great job with it in just a few short months."

Jamie brightened, her tiredness giving way to enthusiasm. "It does look nice, doesn't it? I don't see how they can help but be favorably impressed."

"I don't either, so stop fussing. Go take a shower and relax a little. They won't be here until late this afternoon."

## Love's Gentle Season 143

Jamie shook her head. "I can't. Today is Friday, remember? There's a riding session in—" She glanced at her watch. "Just over an hour. I'll have time for lunch, and that's about it. What about dinner, Gram? Do you need help with it?"

Elinor shook her head firmly. "Absolutely not. I fixed bean salad this morning and set some rolls to rise. All I have to do is fry the chicken and mash the potatoes later."

Jamie's grin widened. "I really should have cooked the meal so they could see what a versatile person I've turned out to be."

"I'll let you do that tomorrow. They're going to stay over the weekend, you know. That will give you plenty of time to show off your cooking skills."

"More than enough," Jamie agreed, going over to the sink to wash her hands. "Matt didn't call, did he?" she asked, hoping her voice sounded casual. Matt had been gone for almost three weeks now. He'd stayed here only long enough to clean up the debris from Edna, then left again for Ocala.

He'd never been gone this long before. But of course, she should have been prepared. He'd told her before he left that he didn't know how long he had to be gone, and probably couldn't get back for some of the riding sessions. She'd had to get another volunteer.

"Nope, he sure didn't. When was he supposed to come home?"

"I don't know, Gram. He didn't say." Elinor's words echoed in her ears, as she dried her hands. She wondered if Matt still considered his place here "home." It was beginning to seem that he didn't, since he was gone so often lately.

She was feeling more and more that he must be planning to move back to Ocala permanently. Of course, he had bought the two hundred acres here. But land could always be sold.

"Well, he'll probably be back soon," Elinor said comfortably, getting sandwich fixings out of the refrigerator. "Be nice if he could meet the family."

"Yes, I guess so." Jamie got out the pitcher of iced tea and poured two glasses. How would her parents react to Matt, she wondered. Would they think he was as great as she did? No, that would be impossible, she decided.

Nothing had changed between her and Matt since the night of the hurricane. They'd worked together to clean up the two farms, assisted by Steve and Carol. Neal, Denise, and several other of the volunteers had also come by and helped get things back in shape for the riding sessions.

The day before Matt's trip, the two of them had fed the horses early and gone to the beach together in the late afternoon. They'd walked and talked on the quiet, uncrowded sugar-white sands, taking deep breaths of the invigorating sea air, listening to the raucous gulls, watching the sea oats swaying in the breeze. Later, they'd watched the sun set over the water, one of the spectacular Florida sunsets. Jamie had felt happy and at peace for those few hours.

Matt had given her a lingering good-night kiss, then told her he was going to Ocala in the morning and he didn't know when he'd be back. He'd asked her if he could leave Sheba with her and Elinor. Since the hurricane, the cat hadn't liked being left alone, he explained.

Jamie had agreed, and now Sheba had practically taken over the household, as cats do. She'd at once laid claim to Elinor's rocker, and now every time Elinor wanted to sit in it, she had to scoop up the cat and hold her on her lap. Not that Elinor minded. No, she was saying she didn't know why she hadn't had a cat for so many years.

With Matt gone, all Jamie's doubts and wonderings had come back. Or maybe they'd never gone away, she thought now, as she sliced tomatoes and washed lettuce leaves. Ted's letter still lay in her dresser drawer. She hadn't answered it, but she hadn't thrown the letter away, either. And she still wasn't sure why.

"Here they are, Gram," Jamie said, her voice a little shaky. She opened the screen door and walked out onto the back porch. A sleek white Lincoln Continental had pulled up into the driveway.

"Mom, Dad!" Jamie ran down the steps and over to the car, a wide smile on her face. She was glad to see them, she really was. She just wished they could approve of the way she wanted to live her life. Maybe after this visit, they would.

Philip Richards got out of the car, returning his daughter's smile. "Jamie, how are you, honey?"

"Fine, Dad." Even in casual slacks and shirt, he looked distinguished, Jamie thought, hugging him. Over her father's shoulder, she smiled at her mother, who'd gotten out of the car and walked around. "Hi, Mom. I'm so glad you could come."

"So are we, dear." Beatrice Richards smiled at Jamie, moving up beside her husband. "You're so lucky the hurricane didn't do more damage. Every time I think of you and Mother staying here instead of coming to us, I shudder."

Jamie hugged her mother too, being careful not to muss Bea's carefully arranged hairdo or her expensive silk shirt. "I know, Mother," she answered. "But we didn't know how close it was going to get to us."

She'd glimpsed a man in the backseat with Linda. She hadn't known her sister was bringing her fiancé, David, along. She hoped her grandmother had fried enough chicken. Then she dismissed that worry. Elinor always fixed more than enough.

"Linda, how nice to see you. And Da—" Jamie's voice stopped dead. The man standing beside her sister, his blond hair gleaming in the afternoon sunlight, his smile confident, wasn't Linda's fiancé.

"Hello, Jamie. It's been a long time." Ted stepped forward, his hand outstretched, his smile widening as he took her unresisting hand in his. "You look wonderful. All this rustic country life must agree with you."

Jamie took a deep, shaky breath and forced her mouth to curve into a smile. "Hello, Ted. Yes, it has been a long time." His hand was warm holding hers, familiar. She remembered the many times he'd taken her hand in his and held it.

"Well, don't everybody stand out there in the hot sun," Elinor called from the back porch. "Come on up here and sit down. I've got iced tea and lemonade."

Somehow Jamie found herself walking with Ted up to the porch, then sitting in the swing with him. The swirling talk went on all around her, but she only half heard most of it. What was Ted doing here with her parents? Did they know that he'd written her that letter? That he wanted to see her again?

As if in answer to her unspoken thoughts, Ted moved a little closer to her on the swing seat. "I wrote you a letter a few weeks ago, Jamie. Did you get it?"

His voice was still familiar too, light and pleasant. "Yes, I got it, Ted," she answered, trying to keep any kind of emotion out of her voice. "I—I didn't know how to answer it."

They seemed to be in a kind of little oasis of quiet, she noticed. Her parents and sister were all talking to Elinor, as if by some unspoken agreement. Maybe she was too suspicious. Maybe it was just a coincidence.

"Well, at least you must have read it, then," Ted said. "I was afraid you wouldn't even do that."

Ted, afraid? That seemed out of character. She gave him a quick glance. His confident expression of a few minutes ago had given way to an anxious one. Jamie blinked, surprise filling her. Ted actually did seem to be sorry for the way he'd behaved three years ago. She shrugged. "Yes, I read it."

After a small silence, he went on, "Have you thought about what I said in it?" His voice sounded almost humble.

Jamie looked at him again, still unable to believe this new Ted. "Yes, I have," she told him quietly. And she had, no matter how many times she'd told herself she wouldn't consider seeing Ted again.

"And have you come to any decisions?" His voice was soft now, still with that almost humble note in it.

Jamie shook her head. "No, I haven't. I—I've been pretty busy," she finished lamely, knowing she was evading the issue.

"Oh, I know that. Bea has told me all the things you've been doing. And then the hurricane too."

"Everybody ready to go eat some fried chicken?" Elinor asked, raising her voice above all the others to be heard.

"You bet, Mom," Philip answered, getting

up at once. "I've been hoping all the way down that that's what you'd cook tonight."

"All that cholesterol!" Bea rolled her eyes in mock horror as she got up too. "But I don't care. No one can cook fried chicken the way you can, Mother."

"Jamie can," Elinor said as everyone came into the big kitchen.

"Jamie?" Linda asked incredulously. "You're talking about my tomboy sister, who never even learned to boil water?" She gave Jamie an arched-eyebrow glance, but her voice had been playful and light. Her dark-brown hair, so like her mother's, was also as expertly arranged. Her face and her brown eyes were carefully made up.

Jamie grinned and shrugged, glad to be in the group and no longer off in the corner with Ted. "That was a long time ago, Linda," she answered. "People do change, you know."

She felt good, suddenly, about the visit, even if Ted had come along. Her family seemed at ease and comfortable, as if they had come just to enjoy the visit with her and Gram. She felt some of her tension ease. Everything was starting off well. She could deal with Ted's presence. And tomorrow, when she showed them around the place, they couldn't help but be impressed with what she'd accomplished.

## *  *  *

Jamie was reading in bed when she heard a soft knock. She slipped into her robe and went to the door.

Ted stood there, in pajamas and robe, a hesitant smile on his face. "Could we talk for a little while, Jamie?" he asked in a low voice.

Since all four of the bedrooms were occupied, Ted was sleeping on the living-room sofa. The house seemed to be quiet—everyone had gone to bed early, tired after the long drive. Jamie realized she'd been half expecting Ted's knock, since there hadn't been any opportunity for them to talk privately all evening. She hesitated, then finally nodded. "All right, let's go to the kitchen."

She followed Ted down the stairs, noticing he was walking as quietly as possible. Maybe she should make some noise, get someone else up. Even while she grimaced at that idea, she knew she wasn't at all sure she wanted to talk to Ted alone. But she'd known this was inevitable ever since she'd seen him get out of the car this afternoon.

"Coffee?" she asked, walking briskly to the stove.

"Not for me, thanks," Ted answered. "I wouldn't sleep if I drank it this late."

"I can make decaffeinated," she suggested,

glad he had sat down at the table and hadn't followed her across the room.

"All right, that sounds good."

Jamie put the kettle on, then measured the coffee, taking as much time as possible. Finally, the coffee made and poured, she sat down across the table from Ted. She stirred milk into her cup, then gave him a casual smile. "So, how are you doing these days?"

Ted looked down at his cup, then shrugged. "All right. I'll be in my third year of medical school in the fall, you know. I'm looking forward to it, but it's going to be rough."

"I imagine so. Are you still planning to specialize in heart surgery?" Jamie knew she was stalling for time. She didn't want the talk to get any more personal than this.

Ted looked up suddenly. "Yes. But I don't want to talk about med school, Jamie. I want to talk about us." He looked at her across the table, his eyes holding her own.

Now Jamie shrugged, moving her eyes away from his, back to her coffee. She picked up a spoon and stirred sugar she didn't really want into it. "I didn't think there was any 'us' anymore, Ted." Why had she said it like that, she wondered as soon as the words were out of her mouth. She *knew* there was no future for them—didn't she?

Ted picked up on her hesitation at once. He reached across the table and covered her hand with his. "I'm not so sure about that, Jamie," he said earnestly. "You said you read my letter. Then you must know I'd like us to start seeing each other again."

Just as earlier today, his hand felt warm and familiar touching her own. What else did it make her feel? Nothing, she told herself quickly, then wondered if that was true. Was she as completely over Ted as she'd thought? She moved her hand away from his, back to her lap, and gave him a straight look. "I don't think that would be a good idea." She made her voice firm and sure, even though she didn't feel that certain inside.

Again, Ted held her gaze. "Are you positive of that? We've both grown up a lot in the last three years. I know I treated you badly, and I'm deeply sorry for it. I'd like to have a chance to prove how different I feel now."

Jamie bit her lip and looked away from Ted's searching glance. Confusion grew inside her. She hadn't thought of Ted for months until she received his letter. It hadn't crossed her mind that he'd ever try to contact her again. Then why hadn't she thrown the letter away at once if she was so positive?

But it was Matt she cared for, wasn't it?

Hard on the heels of that thought came another. She might care for Matt, but she didn't know how he felt about her. A few kisses didn't mean anything, did they? A few dates?

All at once she'd had enough of this. It had been a long, tiring day. She pushed back her chair and got up. She forced a smile onto her face. "This discussion will have to wait until some other time, Ted. I'm too tired to talk about it tonight."

Ted got up too. "All right, Jamie. But I want you to think about what I said. I'm very serious about it."

Jamie nodded as she moved toward the hall. "I'll see you in the morning. Good night." She walked up the stairs to her room, annoyed with herself. Again she hadn't been as positive and firm as she should have, as she'd intended. She'd left the whole thing wide open. Why had she done that? Did she, too, think they might be able to rebuild their relationship on a new, mature foundation?

She stumbled on a step as her eyes blurred from sheer exhaustion. She wasn't going to think about it any more tonight. *But what about Matt?* the sly thought intruded. How did he figure into all this?

Jamie pressed her lips together. If he'd ever stay here long enough for them to get anything settled, she might know how they both felt, she thought crossly, opening her bedroom door.

## Chapter Twelve

Jamie got up at six as usual, still feeling tired. All the unresolved questions had given her a restless night. She fed the horses, then cleaned out the big watering tub, even though it didn't need it. She gave a critical glance around. Everything looked good, she assured herself for the dozenth time.

The fields were still green because they'd had plenty of rain, but by now, in early October, the grass wasn't growing as fast as it had been. There was plenty for another month or two, though, before she'd have to start buying hay. That was fortunate, because her boarders hadn't come in as fast as she'd hoped. And she wasn't giving as many riding lessons as she'd thought she would be by now, either. Money was going to be tight for a while. The familiar knot of tension clenched her stomach muscles. She'd spent a lot more of her savings than she'd planned to.

But the old barn, with its new coat of brick-red paint, looked firm and solid, as if it could outlast several more generations. The horses were sleek and healthy looking. She'd done a lot in a few months, and she felt a good sense of accomplishment as she walked back to the house.

Elinor turned from the stove, where she was frying bacon. "Thought I'd make buttermilk pancakes this morning."

Jamie grinned and rubbed her stomach. "I can't wait! Dad will love them. Mom will complain about calories and cholesterol, and eat them anyway, and so will Linda."

"And what about Ted? Do you think he'll like them?"

Jamie threw her grandmother a quick glance, to find her shrewd dark eyes on hers, a speculative look in them. She'd never told Elinor about Ted's letter, and she knew Elinor was wondering why he was here. She shrugged, feeling her face reddening. "How could he help it?"

"Oh, I don't know. He struck me as the type to probably watch his diet—and his weight. He didn't eat much chicken last night. Jamie, he wrote that letter you got the day of the hurricane, didn't he?"

Jamie sighed. She should have known her grandmother would have figured it out by now.

She went over and poured herself a cup of coffee. "Yes, Gram, he did."

"Did you invite him to come with Bea and Phil?" Elinor deftly turned bacon with a three-tined fork.

"No!" Jamie walked quickly to the refrigerator to take out milk. "I didn't know anything about it."

"Did I smell coffee—and bacon?" Ted appeared in the doorway, fully dressed in jeans and T-shirt, his blond hair brushed, his brown eyes alert and rested.

Jamie swallowed. "You sure did. Good morning, Ted." She managed some kind of a smile. Had he heard what they'd been saying, she wondered. It didn't matter if he had, she decided. He'd brought all this on himself by coming. "Do you want a cup?"

"You won't have to ask me twice!" Ted smiled at both women and took the cup of coffee Jamie handed him. "It was so quiet last night I couldn't sleep. Then in the middle of the night, I heard an awful noise—and the cat decided to sleep with me."

"That was probably a screech owl. Once in a while one will come up from the woods. But I didn't know Sheba was scared of them." Elinor returned Ted's smile.

"Oh, I don't know if she was scared. I think

she just got lonesome. She's not a bad bed partner. At least she doesn't snore."

Jamie gave him a quick glance. Hadn't Ted always thought animals were more of a nuisance than a pleasure? Had he changed that much? Or was this all an act to impress her?

"Good morning, everyone. Mom, I smelled that bacon all the way upstairs. Tell me you're going to make your buttermilk pancakes too?" Philip Richards came into the room, also dressed in jeans and T-shirt.

Jamie stared at her father. He *never* wore jeans. She didn't even know he owned any. Now, if her mother and Linda came down in jeans too, she wouldn't believe it.

They didn't. Bea and Linda appeared a few minutes later, wearing casual slacks and well-tailored shirts. Breakfast was a pleasant meal, everyone enjoying the well-cooked, hearty food, with the conversation general.

Jamie took care to sit across the table from Ted. She wasn't going to give him any opportunities for an intimate talk this morning. As soon as breakfast was cleared away, she suggested she show everyone around.

"And this is the lunge pen we built for training." Jamie's smile felt pasted on, as she turned to her parents. Ted and Linda were behind them. It was only eleven-thirty, but Jamie felt as if she'd put in a long, hard day. Her family had been polite, but they hadn't been impressed by anything they'd seen.

No one said anything for a minute; then Bea laughed lightly. "My, it certainly is rustic, isn't it?" Her voice was condescending.

Jamie took a deep breath, and her spirits plunged even lower as she looked at the pen with her family's eyes. *Rustic* was a kind word for the structure, she decided, even though it had seemed fine to her before. Steve had told her she could get leftover scrap slab boards free from a nearby sawmill. That had been enough for her, and she and Steve had hauled several loads in the truck.

Matt, as usual, had helped with the actual building. Had he, too, thought it looked as shabby as her family did? The uneven-sided slabs were bare of any paint or stain, and most of them still had some of the outer bark left on.

"Yes, I guess it is," Jamie answered, her voice tight. The newly painted barn that had seemed so solid now looked to her as it did to her parents. The paint covered only its underlying, patched-up shabbiness. She squared her shoulders and pointed out the riding group's horses, grazing in the upper fields.

"It's all very worthwhile, Jamie, but maybe

you should wait until you get this place in better shape to do this volunteer work," Linda suggested lightly. "After all, it must take a lot of your time."

"Well, I don't know about the rest of you, but I could use a glass of iced tea," Ted said, filling the awkward silence.

"That sounds like a great idea," Philip put in heartily, his voice a little embarrassed. "I'm not used to all this walking."

"I'm sure Gram has a pitcher of tea in the refrigerator," Jamie answered, trying to lighten her tone. She didn't want her family to know how their complete lack of enthusiasm for everything she was trying to do had affected her. She led the silent group back to the house, wishing the visit was over. How on earth was she going to entertain them the rest of this day and all day tomorrow?

"My, it certainly is humid today, isn't it?" Bea finally said as they came into the yard. "What I wouldn't give for a little air-conditioning right now."

"Oh, it's not bad, Bea," Philip said jovially. "At least it isn't July." He'd tried to be pleasant and polite, for which Jamie was grateful, but she knew he, too, hadn't been impressed with anything she'd done here.

"If it was July, I'd still be in Atlanta," Bea

answered, pushing her hair off her neck. "I don't know how you and Mother stand it here, Jamie. And I suppose you're going to be as stubborn as she's always been about putting in central air-conditioning."

"Mother, I couldn't afford central air-conditioning right now even if I wanted it." Jamie was sorry the minute the words left her lips. She hadn't planned to say anything about her tight finances.

Bea moved closer to her younger daughter and took her arm. "Dear, don't you think you've gone on with this little project long enough? Of course we admire your hard work and determination, but surely by now you can see it isn't going to work out."

Jamie drew a sharp breath. She felt as if her mother had slapped her, but she told herself she would stay calm, she wouldn't lose her temper. Somehow she would be pleasant and polite for the rest of the day and tomorrow when they all left. She moved her arm away from her mother and turned toward her. "No, Mother, I don't see anything of the kind, I—"

Jamie looked up at the sound of a vehicle crunching over the oyster shells of the driveway. Matt's muddy Jeep stood there, and while she watched, her heart skipping a beat, Matt got out and walked toward them. He wore a

## Love's Gentle Season 163

pair of faded old jeans, and a blue T-shirt that brought out the color of his eyes. He'd never looked so good to Jamie, but she wished he were anywhere but here right now.

His eyes swept over the group, resting finally on Ted, who'd moved away from Linda and now stood beside Jamie. Then his eyes met Jamie's, a question in them. She felt her face reddening as Ted slipped his arm through hers in a possessive gesture.

She'd never told Matt about Ted, she realized. Why hadn't she? Because she hadn't been sure she and Ted were really finished? She performed the introductions, and they all walked up on the porch, where Elinor sat. Ted's hand still firmly held Jamie's arm. She had to get him to let go of her!

"I'll get the tea," she said quickly as they all seated themselves. She released her arm from Ted's grasp. "Matt, would you like to help me?" She smiled at him, but his eyes were cold and distant.

"I'll help," Ted put in quickly, before Matt had a chance to answer.

Jamie let out a sigh of frustration as she opened the screen and went inside, Ted close behind her. What a horrible day this was turning out to be! It was bad enough that her family still wouldn't accept what she was doing with her life—that they were still trying to get her to change her mind and leave everything she loved, she thought as she got out the big pitcher of tea. But to have Matt arrive now, at the worst possible time, and misunderstand Ted's presence—that was unbearable.

"Now I understand why you're being so cagey with me, Jamie." Ted's amused voice came from close behind her. "The locals have charms, do they?"

Suddenly his voice sounded just like it had three years ago when she'd told him her plans for her life: amused and slightly scornful, as if what she'd told him wasn't important enough even to discuss seriously. She turned quickly toward him, still holding the pitcher.

That little smile looked just the same too. Ted hadn't changed a bit. Why on earth had she thought he would have? People don't change that easily; she should know from her own experience. *She* hadn't.

She put the pitcher down on the countertop. "You feel just as Mother and Dad do, don't you, Ted?" she asked quietly. "You still think I'm crazy to be here, doing what I'm doing."

Ted's smile faded, and he gave her a wary look. "Surely you can see you don't have much of a future here, compared to what you could have in Atlanta."

"Did you and my parents cook this up between you?" Jamie's voice was still quiet, but tight with anger. "Was this a last-ditch effort to try to make me see the error of my ways?"

Ted shrugged uneasily. "Of course not, Jamie. I—I just came along with them so I could see you." His voice wasn't convincing.

Jamie whirled away to the cabinet where the glasses were kept. She got them out and put them on a tray, then set them down on the countertop. Ted still stood in the same spot, a chagrined look on his face.

"Well, you've seen me. Now you can just go back home with my family and get on with your upwardly mobile life. I'm sure there are any number of other women who'd be delighted to share it with you."

"I see you're still as stubborn as ever. I thought maybe by now you'd have changed."

"The way you've changed?" she asked, raising her brows in disbelief.

Ted's fair skin reddened. "I wasn't lying about how I feel, Jamie. I would like us to get together again."

"But still on your terms, right, Ted? Would you be willing to give up your plans for becoming a big-city specialist and settle for a general practice in the country around here?"

"Don't be ridiculous! That's not a fair comparison at all."

Jamie's glance was straight and firm. "Isn't it? Why not?"

"Why, because it's just not practical, or, or—" Ted sputtered, his face turning a deeper red.

"Need some help in here? We're all dying of thirst." Philip's voice came from the doorway as he shut the screen behind him.

"We're just about to get it ready, Dad." Jamie quickly poured the tea into glasses and added ice cubes. "Here, you can take the tray out, if you want to." Ignoring Ted, she walked out behind her father.

As she came out onto the porch, she heard the sound of a car engine starting, and her heart lurched. Matt was leaving—and she knew he'd reached the wrong conclusions about what was going on between her and Ted. "Couldn't Matt stay?" she asked, turning quickly to Elinor.

Elinor shook her head. "No, he was just stopping by to tell us he has to go back to Ocala this afternoon, and to ask us to keep Sheba for a few more days." Her dark eyes were troubled as they met Jamie's.

"Oh." Jamie took one of the glasses from the tray and sat down in a porch chair beside her mother. A chaotic mixture of emotions filled her, and she couldn't sort them out. At least Ted had gotten her message. He ignored the empty chair beside her and sat down in the swing beside Linda.

"That's a nice young man," Bea said, her voice conciliatory, as if realizing she'd gone too far a few minutes ago. "So he's your next-door neighbor? I was telling him all about how you and Ted were engaged, and that we still had hopes you could patch things up between you."

Jamie felt her blood turn cold in her veins. Things had been bad enough before—now they were hopeless. How could her mother have done such a thing? Did she know she and Matt were attracted to each other, had dated? Had she deliberately tried to mess things up with Matt too?

Suddenly she'd had enough from all of them, especially her mother. She'd interfered in her life for the last time. Jamie got to her feet, her eyes shooting sparks of fire. "Mother, I'm going to tell you this one last time, and that's all. I'm never going to come back to Atlanta to live. I'm never going to go to law school and become a lawyer. Never. Do you understand me?"

Jamie felt tears pricking her eyelids, and she furiously blinked them back as she walked, her back ramrod straight, down the porch steps and rapidly across the yard toward the barn.

"Jamie, wait a minute—" Her mother's agitated voice called to her.

Jamie ignored it and kept going, hoping her mother wouldn't follow her. She didn't want any more talking or explaining. She wanted to be left alone with her horses.

Dusty was in his stall. Jamie went to him, hiding her hot face in the gelding's thick mane.

No one was coming after her, she realized in a few minutes, relieved. She got a bridle and saddle pad from the tack shed, and in a few minutes she was riding down through the lower fields.

A half hour later, she rode back, calmed as she always was after being with the horses, ready to be pleasant and polite for the rest of her family's visit. She'd even apologize for her outburst, but she wouldn't apologize for what she'd said, or back down from her stand. She was finished with worrying about her family's reactions to her life-style.

Elinor was in the kitchen getting lunch. No one else was in sight. Jamie looked around. "Where did everyone go?"

Elinor glanced at her, then smiled wryly. "They all went back to Atlanta, honey."

"Oh, no, Gram!" Jamie said, horrified. "I've

*Love's Gentle Season* 169

spoiled the visit for you, and you hadn't seen them for months. I'm sorry."

"Don't worry about it," Elinor said comfortingly. "They didn't really come down here to visit anyway, you know that."

"No, they came to try to talk me into going back to Atlanta." Jamie's voice was grim as depression hit her. Whom was she trying to convince? The stables weren't a big success. They weren't a success at all. She was just barely hanging on, and that had been obvious to her family.

In spite of the brave words she'd flung at her mother, she wasn't at all sure about what she was going to do, she realized. Maybe her family was right, and she was an idiot to try to struggle on with this stables business. She knew, as well as they did, that most new businesses didn't make it. What had made her think she was any different?

Well, she was doing all she could do to get the business on its feet. She couldn't do anything else there. But maybe she could still catch Matt before he left for Ocala, and try to explain about Ted. She went quickly over to the wall phone and dialed Matt's number. It rang and rang, with no answer, and finally she put the receiver back in its cradle, swallowing a huge lump in her throat.

"He'll be back, honey."

Elinor's sympathetic words didn't make her feel any better. Her depression deepened as she set the table and helped her grandmother finish the meal. Now that it was too late, she knew how she felt about Matt. She loved him, completely, with no reservations. For her, that barrier between them was down at last.

But a lot of good that would do now, because she knew Matt thought she had deliberately deceived him. Would he ever give her a chance to tell him the truth?

## *Chapter Thirteen*

"**W**hoa, Misty," Jamie said soothingly to the jumpy mare. "It's all right." She ran her hands over the mare's sleek rounded sides. Unable to sleep, she had come out to the barn to check on Misty since she was due to foal anytime. Now that time had come—the mare was in labor.

The moon was full tonight, reminding Jamie of that magical evening with Matt at the pond. It bathed the old barn in its soft light, making the flashlight she'd brought along unnecessary. She ran her damp palms down the sides of her jeans, feeling a prickle of nervousness, even though she'd attended many foalings at the horse farm. Everything would probably go smoothly, but she kept remembering all she'd read about the things that could go wrong.

She tightened her lips. At least maybe this would take her mind off her other problems. Three days had passed since the departure of Ted and her family—and Matt. She hadn't been able to shake her depression. Not only had she probably lost Matt, but it also seemed likely that she wasn't going to make it with the stables.

Her rosy-hued glasses had been discarded for good with her family's visit, and now, everywhere she looked, instead of noting the improvements, all she could see were the things that still needed doing—with no money to do them. Everything seemed to be at a standstill.

There were no new boarders, and no one new had called about riding lessons. She couldn't keep on like that over the winter—not with the hay she'd have to buy in addition to the other expenses. She was barely breaking even. If she had any sense at all, she would give up now, before she got in any deeper.

She felt better about only one thing. She'd gotten a letter from her mother yesterday, a letter she still hardly believed the other woman had written.

Her mother had simply and sincerely apologized for bringing Ted with them, and also for leading Matt to believe that Jamie and Ted were going to get back together. Jamie had practically memorized the contents. Her mother had told her she was right to stand up for herself as she had, and that, even though they'd still like to have her in the family law firm, from now on they would accept her decisions about her career and life. She'd ended by asking for Jamie's forgiveness for her interference.

It was ironic that the same events that had finally prompted her family to accept her way of life had also made her see that that life-style just wasn't going to work.

Misty made another restless movement, then turned and nipped at her sides. Jamie bit her lip, her uneasiness growing. She wished Elinor was here, but her grandmother had already gone to bed. No use waking her up unless Misty started having trouble.

She wished *Matt* was here. She tried to push that thought aside, but it kept coming back. She remembered what he'd told her weeks ago: *"Don't worry—if you need me, I'll be just across the fields."* Her mouth twisted. He wasn't just across the fields—he was still in Ocala.

Jamie closed Misty's stall door, then walked down the aisle between the stalls, pausing to say a few words to Dusty and the other horses. She stood in the barn doorway and took a deep breath, trying to calm her jumpy nerves and ignore her urge to call the vet. She couldn't afford his fee, and there was no reason to worry about Misty—nothing seemed to be wrong.

The huge Florida moon made the night almost as bright as day, but Jamie couldn't appreciate its beauty tonight. Prince had come with her, and now he let out a low growl. Jamie felt her heart skip a beat. Prince growled only at strangers. Her glance followed the dog's, and she saw a figure walking across the fields.

She drew a quick breath and put her hand on the dog's head. "It's all right, Prince." Matt. Even if the moon hadn't been full, even at that distance, she'd know his walk anywhere. She hadn't even known he was back from Ocala. Why was he here tonight?

A turmoil of emotions filled her as she watched him rapidly approach. She dreaded seeing him, talking to him, after what had happened a few days ago. But overriding those feelings was relief that he was here—because of Misty. And pure gladness just to see him walking toward her, even if things were hopelessly mixed up between them.

Prince hurried to meet him, ready to apologize for not recognizing him. Matt stopped a few feet from her, his face unsmiling in the moon's silvery beams.

"Hello, Matt. What are you doing here?" Jamie blurted out, then could have kicked herself. That really sounded welcoming, didn't it?

"I don't know. I just somehow got the feeling you needed me, Jamie. Is anything wrong?" His voice was flat, unemotional.

Did he, too, feel the bond between them that she did? Jamie quickly shook her head. "No, nothing's wrong, but I'm glad you're here. Misty's starting to foal." She checked her strong impulse to tell him that wasn't the only reason she was glad he was here.

"I'll take a look at her." He turned and went inside the barn, Jamie beside him. He gave the mare a quick once-over, then turned to Jamie. "You're right. Everything looks fine, though. No cause to worry. You're going to have a foal in a little while."

"Good. Because I sure don't need a vet bill on top of everything else. If she has a good foal, at least I'll be able to make more money when I sell them." Until the words were out, Jamie hadn't known she was going to say them. She bit her lip in chagrin, then glanced up at Matt.

There was emotion on his strong features now. He looked disbelieving and shocked. "You're going to sell out?"

Jamie shrugged. "As my family so clearly pointed out to me a few days ago, it doesn't look as if I have much future here." She remembered her brave words to her mother, about how she'd never leave here, never go to law school. That was all they'd been —words. Words wouldn't pay the bills to keep the stables going.

"I never thought you were a quitter, Jamie."

Matt's deep voice held a disappointed note, and Jamie felt a need to defend herself. "I'm not a quitter—I'm trying to be realistic," she said quickly. "I'm just breaking even here, and most of my savings are gone."

"But you didn't realize that until your family came. Or was it Ted who pointed all this out to you?"

She swallowed. She'd wanted a chance to explain to Matt about Ted. Well, now she had it. But would he believe her? "Matt, there's nothing between Ted and me. Not anymore. It's true we were engaged, but that was three years ago."

Matt's look was straight and unblinking. "Then why did he come here, and why was he hanging on to your arm as if he owned you?"

This wasn't going to be easy. "I didn't even know he was coming. Apparently he and my parents dreamed up some idea of us getting back together."

"You mean you hadn't heard anything from him in three years, and he just came with them and suggested that?" His voice sounded skeptical.

She shrugged uncomfortably. How could she blame him? "Well, not exactly. He wrote me a letter a few weeks ago."

"And you didn't think maybe you should tell me about it? Or about Ted, for that matter?" He didn't sound any more convinced than a few moments ago.

All at once the whole scene was too much like the ones she'd had to go through with her parents for years. Defending herself, explaining herself. To a man who'd never given her any indication he had serious feelings about her.

Jamie's eyes shot sparks at him. "Why should I have? There's nothing between you and me but a few dates, is there? We're not committed to each other."

His expression changed, and she couldn't read the new look in his eyes. After a moment, he nodded. "You're right, Jamie. We're not committed to each other at all. But I—"

Misty let out a grunting sound, and Matt turned quickly to her. In a moment he turned back to Jamie. "She's about ready to foal." His words were clipped and firm, everything else but the job at hand wiped away from his face.

Jamie pressed her lips together, pushing their private problems to the back of her mind so she could concentrate on what had to be done if Misty had some kind of trouble.

But the foaling went smoothly, and within an hour Misty produced a beautiful dark gray filly. They stood by to help if the baby had trouble nursing, but after a few fumbling attempts, the tiny, wobble-legged creature was successful, and began nursing frantically.

"Oh, Matt," Jamie said, caught up in the wonder of the birth. "She's so beautiful. I've watched this a dozen times before, but it's always so wonderful to see the new little life. And this one's extra special—she's mine!"

"I know. It's like a miracle every time it happens." His voice was soft and almost reverent too, as they watched the mother and baby.

Gradually the foal's long, wobbly legs firmed, and Jamie felt something in her heart firming too. What she'd blurted out to Matt a moment ago was so true, she ached inside. This foal was special because it was hers. She belonged here. She couldn't leave here. No matter what.

They left the new mother and baby and walked outside. Prince had waited for them beside a bench, and now he raised his head, wagging his tail in greeting. The moon bathed the whole landscape in its silvery, magical light.

Jamie drew a deep breath and turned to Matt. "I'm going to stay, Matt. I don't know how I'll do it, but I can't leave. Everything I love is here." He didn't know how true that was, she thought. *Everything* she loved was

## Love's Gentle Season 179

here—including the man she loved with all her heart.

She walked over and sat down on the bench, and Matt joined her. "I've finally realized I no longer have to prove myself to my family," she said, "but I'm glad they finally can accept the way I choose to live my life." She told Matt about the letter she'd received from her mother.

How she wished she could share her life with Matt, but since that wasn't possible, then she would at least have the rest of the life she loved. Somehow she'd manage to keep the stables going.

Matt was silent for a long moment. "I was hoping you might want to do a little more than that with your life," he said finally.

She gave him a quick, stunned look. Was Matt also turning traitor? Did he, too, believe she couldn't make a go of the stables, despite what he'd just said a few minutes ago? She'd hoped to keep him as a good friend at least, if they could never be anything more.

He reached over and took her unresisting hand in his, a warm smile curving his mouth. "What I mean is, I was hoping you might have included marrying me in your plans for the future."

Jamie blinked, her eyes widening. "You

want to marry me? But why didn't you ever say anything—" Her voice faltered. She felt a bubble of joy rising inside her, banishing the sadness.

Matt's strong hand squeezed her smaller one. "Believe me, I realized when I saw you with Ted that I should have. But I knew there was still something you had to settle for yourself—in your own mind. You had all these unresolved feelings toward your family, but I felt there was something else.

"When I saw you with Ted—well, I thought that was it. You still cared for him, and I was out in the cold. You can't imagine how relieved I felt a few minutes ago when you told me that was all over for good."

Jamie nodded, and her eyes began to shine, the joy she felt strengthening. "I know. I had that feeling too. I guess I wasn't sure about a lot of things, including Ted, and just didn't realize it until I saw him again. But I'm completely sure now—about everything."

"Does that include me?" Matt asked. "You still haven't answered my question."

Her mouth curved into a smile as she looked into Matt's moon-washed face. "Yes, I'll marry you, Matt." Happiness filled her. Then a sudden sobering thought struck her. "But how can we—I mean, I can't give up my sta-

## Love's Gentle Season     181

bles, and you're going to sell your place here and move back to Ocala."

He gave her an astonished glance. "Where did you get that idea?"

She shrugged, the happiness creeping back. "Well, you've been gone so much lately. I thought you'd decided you couldn't run both places from here."

"You're right—I came to the same conclusion a few weeks ago. That's why I've been gone so much lately—I decided to sell the Ocala ranch."

"You sold the Ocala ranch?" Jamie echoed him in disbelief.

He nodded. "Yes, I signed the closing papers yesterday. With the two hundred acres I bought here, and some more land nearby I plan to buy, I can do all I want to right here. I've done nothing but work at building up that Ocala ranch since I was sixteen. Now I want time to do a few things I enjoy." He reached out and drew Jamie to him. "And I want to do them with you. Because I love you, Jamie."

She sighed contentedly and snuggled into the curve of his shoulder. Her head fit exactly, as if it were made to order. "I love you, Matt." Then she moved back and looked up at him, a frown between her brows. "But I want to keep on running the stables and working with the riding group," she told him, a touch of the old stubborn defiance in her voice.

Matt grinned as he tilted her face up. "Naturally. I plan to help you with all those things. Why do you think I was trying to make myself indispensable to you?"

"I just thought you were being a good neighbor," she said teasingly as his head bent down to hers.

"I plan to be a lot more than a good neighbor to you, Jamie Richards," he said softly. "I've loved you since that first day when I helped you repair the stall."

"I think I've always loved you too, Matt Douglas," Jamie murmured, moving to meet him halfway.

The moon shone down upon them like a benediction as they exchanged a long, lingering kiss. A cool autumn wind blew across the wide field. Summer was over, but the magic of their love was real, and would last through all the seasons.